Always and Forever Be Mine

by

Dilys J Carnie

This is a work of fiction. Names, characters, places, and incidents are either the product of the author's imagination or are used fictitiously, and any resemblance to actual persons living or dead, business establishments, events, or locales, is entirely coincidental.

Always and Forever Be Mine

Cover Art by *Tina Lynn Stout*

The Wild Rose Press, Inc.
PO Box 708
Adams Basin, NY 14410-0708
Visit us at www.thewildrosepress.com

Publishing History
First Edition, 2023
Trade Paperback ISBN 978-1-5092-4999-2
Digital ISBN 978-1-5092-5000-4

Previously Published 2017 Beachwalk Press
Published in the United States of America

"But Aunty Tally…our Christmas tree," a voice piped up in the back seat.

Talia could tell from Charlie's tone that he was on the verge of tears, and her heart broke for him. Turning her head so she could see him, Talia smiled at him. "We'll go get one later on the bus."

She hoped she'd be a little more steady by then. The incident with Roy had shaken her up, and if she was honest, it had frightened her. She'd been so grateful when Max had come to stand beside her.

"I'll take you to get one," Max said.

"Yes, yes, yes. Please, can we go with Max?" Charlie pleaded as he jumped up and down in his seat.

"You don't have to." She was thankful that he hadn't said anything about the altercation that had just occurred.

"No, I don't, but I want to, and perhaps later you can explain why that man was shouting at you?"

He had lowered his voice toward the end of his words, and she looked at him, about to argue, but she could see in his face that he wasn't going to take no for an answer. But she didn't owe him anything…yes, she did, and to be honest, it would be nice to share it with someone.

She stared back at Max as he waited for her answer. He had started the car, and she could feel the full force of the heater on her body as it finally thawed out.

"Thank you. It certainly would be easier than the bus." Talia had not been looking forward to doing that.

"Perhaps we could get something to eat as well. Are you hungry, Charlie?" Max asked her nephew.

Dedication

To my baby girl. I salute you for the woman you have become, the courage you have shown, and the love you give.

Chapter 1

Max Harvey looked out of the hotel window. The whiteness of the snow on the ground glistened in the winter sunshine like sparkling diamonds. It was almost Christmas, a time of year he loved despite his childhood. There was something very magical and honest about how people became with their generosity and happiness that permeated the air.

He usually spent the holiday at the cabin in the mountains with his friends, but this year Jarrod had married and Liam had to stay in the city to work on an important case. So perhaps it was just as well that he had to hop on a flight from DC to the UK last minute to help solve the problems with the new design he'd been working on for the wings of a new airplane for the government.

Max turned to pick up his briefcase before heading to the door. Opening it, he stepped out into the hallway and something plowed into him with the force of a hurricane. His back hit the door as it closed behind him, and he grabbed hold of the person's shoulders to stop them from falling to the floor.

The scent of roses on a summer's day permeated his senses. A woman lifted her face from his chest, and her short, layered, honey-blonde hair was tucked behind tiny ears, the lobes covered with small gold studs. Her heart-shaped face was pale, with shadows beneath her amber-

1

colored eyes. In fact, behind the round glasses she wore he noticed how amazingly deeply tinted her eyes were.

"I'm so sorry. Are you okay?" Her English accent sounded breathless, and before he'd had a chance to speak she had twisted free of his grip on her arms.

"Did I hurt you?" he asked.

"No, I'm fine, and you?"

"I'm fine too."

She moved behind a cleaning trolley, and he realized she was the hotel maid. She wore a black tunic with matching pants. She was slim, and he estimated her height at around five foot eleven, but her amber eyes, which had flecks of gold, fascinated him.

"I can come back to clean your room later?" she said.

"No, go for it. I'm on my way out anyway. Let me get the door for you." Max swiped his card and it clicked. He stood aside while holding the door open for her.

"Thank you," she said, walking past him and into the room.

He couldn't think of anything else to say to her, so he let the door close behind him. It was a strange encounter, and what was going on with his heart rate?

Despite a childhood that didn't hold much love, his persona was trusting and his heart gave. He just hadn't found a woman to share the life he'd made for himself. It was probably because he was cautious with his heart. He loved women, but a relationship had been missing from his life for a while,

His reaction to the maid was ridiculous, entirely too unnerving, which he didn't understand. Standing at the elevator, he pressed the button and waited for it to reach his floor. When the doors opened, Max stepped inside.

Pressing the button for the ground floor, he shoved his hand into his wool overcoat, deciding that whatever he felt was ridiculous.

The doors opened into the hotel lobby, and he headed straight to the exit which led outside into a busy street. It was still snowing. He pulled up his coat collar as a gust of cold winter air hit him square in the face.

"Taxi, sir?" The porter stepped toward him.

"Yes, please."

Within seconds a cab pulled up to the curb, stopping beside him.

"Thank you." He looked at the name tag on the porter's uniform. "Jim." He gave him a five-pound note.

"Thank you, sir." He tipped his hand to his cap as he opened the car door for Max.

"Hawarden Airport, please. Take me to the Broughton factory on-site."

Max set his briefcase on the seat beside him. The new and improved designs inside were secret; the talks he'd had with the British government and the US were going to be overseen by the British engineers.

The design would be added to all fighter jets in both countries. It wasn't anything out of the ordinary for Max to be working on top-secret work, and he was proud of his achievements. Liam and Jarrod, his friends from his time spent in a children's home, had also achieved good things. All of them were at the top of their careers.

Even after all these years, they were still best friends. They had shared some wild times growing up, but they'd stuck together. They could have easily gone down that slippery slope of feeling resentful, blaming everyone else for how messed up they were.

But they'd given each other a kick up the ass and

gone on to become the best in their chosen occupations. Jarrod's building company was worth millions, and Liam was a criminal attorney who owned his own practice. Max, an aero engineer, had written several books on the subject of aerospace, as well as designing some of the most advanced wings for secret government air supports.

Max also lectured at Georgetown College in DC, a job that he loved. Nothing was more satisfying than educating a young person in a subject that was very close to his heart. He never thought in a million years he would like lecturing, but somehow it gave him an innate sense of achieving something that felt good.

It was a short ride from the hotel to where he needed to be. The cab stopped at his destination and Max got out, shivering at the momentary change in temperature from the warm taxi to the cold air outside.

He paid the driver and then made his way to the unit that held his design. His feet crunched on the fresh snow, and his insides churned a little as they always did when he would be faced with something he had designed.

He would be there for the day, he had no doubt about that, but he was looking forward to seeing how far they had gotten with the design that had taken him the best part of three years to perfect.

* * * *

That evening Talia Wolf sat at her kitchen table, exhausted, bills scattered across the surface. It didn't matter how long she stared at them, it was getting harder and harder to cover them all. She'd used all her savings to help with Tilly's nursing care. Her parents, it seemed, had used everything they had to help with Tilly's acting career…even sold the house.

Meow.

She looked down to see Molly pushing herself against her leg, her little tail up. Talia bent down and gathered her up in her arms. At the minute, she could barely afford to feed herself and Charlie, but when this little thing had shown up on her doorstep, shivering in the cold, she hadn't had the heart to close the door without bringing her in.

"Hey, little kitty. I wish life were as simple as you are," she said as she stroked the black ball of fur on her lap who was trying to pull out the toggle attached to her sweater. "Hey no," Talia said as she lifted the small cat and buried her face in the fur. It was soft, and she loved how it felt against her skin. The cat had put some weight on in the short time since Talia had rescued her. "Do you want some milk?"

Molly purred as if to say yes.

Talia went to the refrigerator and took the milk carton from the shelf. Placing her on the floor, she poured the liquid into her dish. "Here you go," she said as she set the plate down. The cat lapped it up, purring at the same time.

Two things in her life kept her going. One was her sister Tilly. Although Tilly couldn't communicate anymore, it was just having her there, and knowing she was doing her very best to make things as comfortable as possible for her twin. The other was her five-year-old nephew Charlie. They'd almost been strangers until the accident, but now he was her world.

Talia's biggest regret was that she had to work so many hours, although she had managed to take Christmas off. It was important for her to do that as it was their first time together. Charlie's Santa Claus list was long, and she tried her best to get everything.

Tomorrow was her day off, and she was happy to spend it with her nephew. They were going to find a Christmas tree. Her brow creased. It unnerved her that their future was so up in the air. Talia had always known what she wanted to do, and planned it down to the last letter. Her life. Her career. Her future.

Going upstairs, she went into the little boy's room where she could hear a slight snore. It made Talia smile. Charlie had been fast asleep when she'd come home tonight. Mrs. Sweet, her next-door neighbor who picked Charlie up from school, had given him his tea. Leaning down, she brushed his soft hair back from his forehead and kissed his cheek.

Talia wouldn't be able to manage without Mrs. Sweet. Well, she would, but it would have meant she'd have to pay for extra after-school care. Talia tried to get home most nights before Charlie went to sleep, but on this occasion, she hadn't been able to.

Going back downstairs, she switched the kettle on and took a mug from the cupboard, leaning against the countertop while she waited for the water to boil. Her phone started to ring and she put her hand into her trouser pocket to fetch it.

She looked at the screen. It was April. "Hi," she said as she answered the call.

"Hey, Talia. How are you?"

"Like I permanently want to toss up my stomach contents, and you?"

"Never mind about me. This is the second time you've moved in eleven months. You have to stop hiding, deal with it head-on."

"I can't," she said as her stomach churned inside out.

6

"I can't take the chance that he might find us."

"Has he tracked you down at all in the last six months?"

"No."

"So, I don't think he is about to now."

"You don't know that, April. He's Charlie's dad, another one of Tilly's mistakes," she said of her sister.

"I understand, Talia, I really do, but it can't be good for Charlie to be moving around so much. You'll be safe where you are, the house is hidden away."

Talia shivered as a wave of sheer panic inundated her. "I hope you're right. I do know it's unsettling for Charlie. He needs stability, and I'm struggling to give him that."

"Hey, don't think like that. You're doing a great job. It wasn't your fault, Talia…you know that, right?"

"I know it wasn't my fault, but perhaps if I'd come home more…"

"And how would that have helped?"

"I might have been able to stop Tilly from marrying a drug addict."

"You and I both know that when Tilly decided to do something, nothing would stop her."

April was right, that was just the way her sister was.

"You're a good friend," she said as she put a teabag from the canister into her cup and poured the boiling water over it.

Talia had been thrown into a world of parenting, and her skills were zilch. She didn't have the know-how to look after a child of any age. Now ask her about fossil remains or buried artifacts and she would be top of the class. But she'd had to give that up; traveling worldwide was not an option with a five-year-old child to look after.

"We help each other out, always have. That's what friends do for each other, Talia."

Taking the stewed teabag out, she took the milk out of the refrigerator and put a splash into the boiling liquid before returning it. For a moment, she stared at the steam and sighed deeply. The difference from her life before to now was enormous.

April had been her best friend since starting in school. Talia had been the only child who sat in the corner with small round glasses on and her thumb in her mouth while everyone danced around Tilly.

"It will get better. You know it will. It's only been eleven months."

"I liked my life before all of this."

"I know, honey, but that was a life where you knew nothing but work. You were obsessed. Nothing else mattered when you were on a dig."

"I loved my work. I was good at it."

"I'm sorry about what has happened to you. It was a massive blow when the accident happened, and the loss of your parents…"

Yeah, it was. Her mum and dad had died in the car crash that had left her twin sister brain damaged and paralyzed. Talia had been on a dig in Greece, doing what she loved most, finding ancient objects, bones, anything with a history.

"I'm so mad at myself."

"Talia Wolf, shut up this minute. I don't want to hear that. You have nothing to be mad about. It wasn't your fault."

"I should have been there."

"And done what? Got killed in a road accident…then who would be there for Charlie?"

"But I'm hopeless with him."

"I've seen you with him. You're a mum in the making and don't let anyone tell you otherwise."

She giggled at her friend's stern voice. She could imagine her bright red hair piled at the top of her head with several pens sticking out of the strands as she marked her pupil's books.

"Yes, miss," she said.

"Umm…you better believe it. You're going through a rough time, but I believe it will improve. It's different than what you are used to, but you're good at solving problems, and your patience is endless."

"What if I can't keep Charlie safe?"

A silence ensued for several seconds. "You think that Roy will take him from you?"

"Yes. I don't know what he will do to him. He had no problems beating Tilly up…it was his fault they were in the car when it crashed. If she hadn't been trying to get away from him…" Her mouth was dry at the thought and she took a sip of tea before sitting down.

"I'm sure that Roy has long since gotten bored of trying to find you. You know the drugs he does…they've wiped out any brain cells he might have had."

"I never wanted kids; it wasn't in my future," Talia piped up.

"Because you were immersed in your job, Talia, and let's face it, you don't want to share yourself with anyone."

"Tilly was the pretty one, she was the one that the men liked. I'm too plain and cold for relationships." She'd had a few boyfriends but nothing that she could call a relationship.

"Now you're just being hard on yourself, but I'm not

going to argue with you. Deep down, you know that none of that is true and only you think it."

"Why did this have to happen? Tilly made me guardian of her son and the selfish part of me hates her for it, then I hate myself for thinking like that."

"Look, whatever you think of yourself, you have a responsibility. You didn't choose for this to happen, but you are a good person, Talia, and Tilly knew that, it's why she did what she did. She knew if anything happened to her you would make Charlie your number one priority. Listen." April's voice softened. "I've got to go, but we'll meet up soon, and if you need to talk, ring me anytime, day or night…promise me you will?"

"I will. Thanks, April." She hung up, setting her phone on the table, cradling her drink between her hands.

Talia promised herself that she would do anything to protect Charlie, and she'd keep that promise for her whole lifetime.

* * * *

Max handed the valet the keys to the car he had rented when he realized he would be staying in the UK a lot longer than he had anticipated. The designs needed to be adjusted before they made any more changes to the airplane he had helped design.

The doorman opened the glass door and Max walked inside, thanking the man who stood in a gray uniform and peaked cap. The opulence of the lobby was extravagant and the epitome of English history. As he passed the desk clerk, he gave a small wave and headed for the elevator. Entering, he pressed the button for his floor. When the elevator stopped and the doors slid open, Max strode down the hall to his room, breathing a sigh of relief as he walked inside.

He tossed his coat on the bed and loosened his tie, opening the top button. It had been a long day, and he was still feeling the effects of jet lag. He went to the mini-bar and poured himself a scotch, downing the fiery liquid in one go. It warmed him inside and out.

The snow had been relentless all day. He'd passed several gritters and snowplows on his way back to the hotel. He hoped it would let up, otherwise he would be stranded in the hotel and he didn't have time for that. Sitting on the small sofa in his executive room, he switched the TV on, flicking to the news channel.

But while watching the news his mind drifted to this morning when he'd bumped into the maid. Those glasses she wore did her no favors, because she had the most amazing amber eyes. They were very expressive. Short, honey-blonde hair that had the odd strand of a lighter shade.

A slim-built woman, the uniform she wore hid what looked to be a good figure. When she had bumped into him he'd felt the cushioning of large breasts and he had barely managed to keep his gaze off them, but he'd so wanted to look.

It caused a punch of sexual desire that had been forceful enough to make him lose his concentration, and that seldom happened. He was good at focusing and not letting anything distract him. But she could distract him anytime. *That's such a typical male thought*, he scolded himself.

One of the things that he'd promised himself was that nothing would stand in his way of achieving all he wanted to, and nothing did. His work was important to him, and he'd worked hard to get where he was today.

His mom died when he was born, and his dad died

when he was fourteen. He was an only child with no other family, so he'd been put into the childcare system. Max had been too old for foster parents to want him, so he'd ended up in a children's home, where he'd met Liam and Jarrod seventeen years ago, and they were still great friends.

Max's mind wandered back to the maid from this morning. He wondered what her story was. She'd actually made him think for a moment about something other than aerospace designs. What was it about her that didn't fit the uniform she wore? And he didn't mean figure-wise. But he couldn't put his finger on what it was.

Setting his glass on the small table in front of him, he toed his shoes off. Lifting his legs, he lay full length on the sofa. His legs were hanging over the edge, but Max was too exhausted to care. He should have been thinking about work, but all he could think about were those mesmerizing eyes, her slim body against his, and other entirely selfish things. And if he was honest, a bit lecherous. He felt his sleepiness overtake him and he allowed it.

When he next opened his eyes, Max looked at his watch. Holy hell, it was 6:30 AM. He'd slept on the sofa all night. His neck was stiff as he swung his feet to the carpeted floor and drew his fingers through his hair. He must have been exhausted to have slept all night without even getting into bed.

He had a headache from hell. Max went into the bathroom and turned on the shower. Stripping, he stepped into the large cubical, hoping it would ease the ache at his temples. Max hissed out a breath when the water hit him, his body aching from a night on the sofa.

Max grabbed a towel and wrapped it around his waist when he finished.

Going over to the hotel phone, he called down for breakfast and coffee to be delivered to his room. By the time it came he was dressed and ready for the busy day ahead. He poured some coffee from the cafetière and walked over to the window. It was still dark, but he could see the wintery weather's whiteness with the streetlights' help. It had snowed heavily through the night, but the road outside the hotel was clear.

When he'd ordered breakfast, Max had asked for his car to be brought by the hotel at eight o'clock. Picking up his cell to look at his emails, he could see from the time there were still twenty minutes to go.

He had a text message from Jarrod asking him what he was doing at Christmas. Max knew that Maisy wanted him to go to their house for the holiday and she would have pestered Jarrod to find out what he was doing. She liked to mother him although they were the same age. Watching Jarrod scowl at him when he wasn't getting attention from his wife was fun.

Max had been delighted that they were expecting their first baby together. It had been extra special because Maisy hadn't known if she wanted to have more babies after losing her own. But you only had to see the happiness on both their faces to know how thrilled they were. It had been an extraordinary pleasure when they had told him, especially as he and Liam were asked to be godparents.

After dealing with a few important emails, he poured himself another cup of coffee. He quite possibly would end up spending Christmas here in the UK. The thought didn't fill him with pleasure, but it was important to get the design to work. The problem lay with the aerodynamics of the wing structure, and they needed less drag on it.

He'd worked on the blueprints yesterday and was anxious to get to the factory to see if his improvements would make the difference they needed. He drank the last of his coffee before putting on his coat. Picking up his briefcase with his laptop and designs inside, he was about to leave the room when his cell rang. It was Jarrod. Max thought about not answering because he knew Maisy would be disappointed if he couldn't make it for Christmas. Especially as her parents would be visiting her from England.

At nearly four months pregnant she was very emotional, but he didn't think it was because she was expecting but rather because it brought back memories of the two children she'd lost. He couldn't imagine what that had been like for her. She was so lovely inside and out, and his friend Jarrod was besotted with her.

He swiped across the screen and answered the call.

"Hey, Jarrod."

"It's not Jarrod, it's me," Maisy said, the very quaint tones of her British accent sounding in his ear.

"Maisy, how are you?" Max asked.

"I'm fine. I just wanted to know about Christmas. It's only two weeks away."

"Honestly, I don't know. If I can sort things out here, I'll be home, but it's gonna be last minute either way."

"That's fine." There was disappointment in her voice, and he hated that. "I'll assume you'll be here, and if you can't make it, I'm sure Jarrod will have no problem consuming your share of the food."

He heard some noises in the background suggesting

that Jarrod would indeed have no qualms about doing that.

"I'll pass you on to Jarrod now. Take care."

"I'll talk to you soon, Maisy."

"You better," she said before he heard what sounded like the noise of his friend and her kissing as he waited with the phone to his ear. Really, they couldn't keep their hands off each other.

Jarrod was so much in love with Maisy. Max felt a slight tightness in his chest because he was envious of his friend, but they were like brothers and he was happy for him. Jarrod had a dreadful childhood, and he deserved to be happy.

Max hadn't chosen to be single, but he had been so intent on being successful that it was only now that he thought of being with someone. He guessed he was a little like his dad, not so much a mad scientist but a mad designer. He laughed to himself.

"Hey, I'm still here," he said as he put the phone on speaker and walked to the window. "When you two have finished being all lovey-dovey with each other."

"Sorry, bud. How's it going there in the UK?" Jarrod asked.

"Not bad. There's a problem with the aerodynamics. The angle of attack is wrong for the efficiency needed."

"Okay, dude, that just went way over my head. For future reference, try to give me an easier description when I ask about your work. That's like me telling you that many different types of pine wood are determined by density and strength."

Max chuckled. "Got ya," he said. "The weather is a bitch here. It's snowed the whole time I've been here, and it's not letting up."

"Good old British weather," Jarrod said.

"Umm, seems so. I'm guessing you didn't call to talk about the weather."

Jarrod laughed. "No, I got bombarded with questions from Maisy about you, so I figured I'd let her call you."

"Ha, thanks for that, bud," he said, knowing Jarrod was teasing. "I take it Liam is retreating to the cabin," he said about the place the three of them had invested in some time ago.

"You know he is. Even Maisy couldn't persuade him to stop his yearly hibernation."

"He always has hated Christmas," Max said.

"Can you blame him?"

"Nope. Anyway, I gotta get going, I have a meeting at nine AM. I'll let you know as soon as I can about Christmas."

"No worries, buddy."

The call ended and Max put his phone in his coat pocket before picking up his briefcase. At that moment, a bird landed on the windowsill, and they stared at each other. He was kinda cute with a red breast, and very festive to look at, but Max had no idea what type of bird it was. It left as quickly as it came, and Max turned from the window, making his way to the door.

It was quiet when he stepped out of his room and walked down the corridor. He was a little disappointed that the maid who had given him thoughts of desire wasn't anywhere to be seen. The plush, red carpeting silenced every step he took. Max took a right turn leading to the elevator and smacked into something soft. He automatically reached out, his hands going around a slim waist, and he caught a whiff of something sweet and spicy. Max recognized that scent from yesterday. It was the maid with the beautiful amber eyes. He felt her fingers on his chest.

"This is becoming a habit," he drawled as he watched the fair skin of the woman he'd bumped into yesterday go the color of the bird's breast he'd seen earlier. He hadn't appreciated how much he enjoyed the scent of a woman, especially this one. Max was so busy building a career and reputation over the years. He hadn't given himself the time to explore something more from a woman, and it had eluded him until now. "Are you okay?" he asked.

She nodded. Max couldn't help the satisfaction he felt at her closeness. His gaze dropped to her mouth, the little breaths sexy in their entirety, her lips pink and glistening just as the tip of her tongue licked them.

Good Lord, she was going to feel how completely aroused he was in a minute, so he stepped back, glad that he had an overcoat on. The maid stepped back as well, crouching down to pick up the spilled contents of her basket that he hadn't even seen he'd knocked over.

"Let me help you with that."

"No, really it's fine."

But he ignored her protest and bent down to help her until everything was back in her basket.

"Max Harvey," he said, putting his hand out to shake hers as they stood up together.

It seemed as though she wasn't going to give her name, but then she took his outstretched hand and shook it. "I'm Talia Wolf."

"Pretty name," he said as her fingers wrapped around his before letting go.

"Thank you," she said.

They stood for a moment studying each other, and then she grabbed hold of her trolley, pushing it past him and around the corner. He couldn't help himself from turning around and staring after her, only to find she was doing the same thing. She nearly tripped over her feet when she saw him looking at her.

He chuckled.

It had made his day to see her again. Max couldn't understand what was so different about this woman, but she made him smile and he wanted to learn more about her.

He would, even if it meant waiting to go out at this time every day so he could bump into her again, accidentally or on purpose.

Chapter 2

Talia stepped out of the hotel's back entrance and took a deep breath, watching it spiral out in front of her when she released it. Lifting her face, she allowed the large, soft snowflakes to settle on her hair and skin before she slipped her hat on.

The beauty of each particle of ice fascinated her in its organic form; no two the same. The one she caught in her hand stayed in shape until it melted into a sliver of water.

She shivered and quickly put on her gloves, huddling into her large green scarf. The snow was unusual though not impossible at this time of year, but she couldn't remember the last time the UK had such a cold winter.

Talia hoped to go Christmas tree shopping today, but someone had called in sick and work asked if Talia would go in. She couldn't refuse...the extra money was needed.

The streets of Chester were covered white with frosted crystals sparkling in the streetlights. It was easy to see how deadly they would be under one's feet. Her old car had decided in its infinite wisdom to refuse to start this morning, and eventually, after repeatedly trying to start it, she had sucked all the power out of the battery. She'd known that she was on borrowed time with it.

So, it would be a bus until she could come up with

the funds for the repairs, and she had added expense buying Charli'e Christmas gifts. It would be well into the new year before she had enough to fix it.. She wasn't precisely delighted at having to use the bus service. It was a five-minute walk to Foregate Street, where she would get the bus home to the cottage where she was staying with Charlie. He was so excited about Christmas. He'd written his letter to Santa ages ago, but he kept adding to his list, and each time he did that they had to write another letter to Father Christmas.

This time last year they had spent it as a family, although Tilly had only stayed for Christmas Eve and then she had left, saying she had an important date that would help with her acting. Yeah, Talia believed her.

Just like that, Tilly had left her son Charlie with her parents. Her sister had been a terrible mother, and it was sad that Charlie missed his grandparents more. She'd taken him to see his mum at the care home, but Charlie had refused to go again, and she hadn't pushed it.

Slowly, she was trying to put their lives back together. The determination and effort it took were exhausting, but she was more than used to keeping her emotions in check. Since the accident, she had to become a mum, dad, and grandparent. At times it was very overwhelming. For one scary moment, she could feel those feelings sneak out of the box she had duly kept them in but she quickly shoved them back in.

Talia approached the bus stop. A few other people were waiting, and she stood in the line, her feet sinking into the soft snow that covered the pavement completely, each footstep made disappeared with the falling flakes. Within minutes of standing there, the bus slowed down at the stop. Once inside, she took a seat by the window for the short ride.

Talia couldn't help the yawn that escaped her. Her work at the hotel was far more exhausting than being on a dig looking for artifacts for eighteen hours a day. She'd just done an eight-hour shift, and she could hardly keep her eyes open. Looking at her watch, Talia hoped she would be home in time to tuck Charlie into bed and read him a story.

He was such a sweet little thing, definitely Tilly's son to look at, but those that didn't know her sister would say that she was his mum. Despite being twins, they weren't identical but looked like sisters.

Tilly had been the dramatic one and had liked the attention, with a great nightlife included, while Talia was so different it was as if they were on opposite sides of the spectrum. They say most twins are best friends, but they weren't. Still, Talia visited her sister every week—or tried to, she wasn't always successful—but Tilly didn't recognize her.

Talia's mind wandered to her encounters with the stranger at the hotel, and her stomach felt funny, almost like there were hundreds of butterflies inside, flapping their wings insistently, softly. That was really weird! She frowned at her reaction to a man she didn't even know. She'd never felt chemistry with the opposite sex, so this surprised her.

He had the most amazing navy-blue eyes, and his black hair was graying at the temples, but his short, dark beard was fascinating to her. It made him look slightly piratic, sending a tingle through her body. He towered over her five feet eleven height.

Talia sighed. She was always more interested in the dead than the living. The older, the better.

Talia had always been the dowdy one out of the twins. Tilly had been beautiful and highly spoilt. Talia always spoke her mind, and Tilly said what everyone wanted to hear. Unless you knew, no one would ever have guessed they were twins.

She got up from her seat as the bus slowed down at her stop. Hanging onto the rail, she moved down the aisle and stepped off the step onto the snow-filled pavement, shivering as a blast of cold air hit her. Shoving her hands in her pockets, she waited for the bus to pass before crossing the road.

There wasn't much automotive traffic tonight, and she stepped onto the road. She was glad that the streetlights were working. It was eerie on this side of town where there weren't many houses. Trees surrounded the cottage Talia had rented. It was the perfect place for someone who didn't want to be found, and she didn't

Although the main roads were gritted, the surface was still slippery. As she stepped off the pavement to cross to the other side, Talia could feel her feet sliding from beneath her. And like a rag doll, she fell hard on her bottom. Talia heard a car stop beside her. Shit, she could have quite easily been beneath those wheels.

Someone peered down at her, and for a moment a sliver of fear went through her before she looked up and saw it was the man from the hotel. She gave a weak smile as her feet slithered and skated while she tried to get back onto her feet. When she nearly fell again, the man grabbed hold of her arms.

"Are you okay?" he asked as he helped her get up.

"Yes, thank you, apart from a bruised bottom, it's big enough to stand the pain." She tried to laugh off the whole thing while setting her askew glasses back on her nose.

The man chuckled, and Talia squirmed in embarrassment. She was so, so glad that she had trousers on.

She didn't think he recognized her, but why would he? She wasn't very memorable. She managed to stay on her feet with his reassuring hands on her arms.

"Thank you," she said as she dusted the snow from her coat.

"Do you live far?" he asked.

"No, just across the road," she replied, trying not to stare into those fascinatingly dark, smoky eyes. It was hard not to notice the sexy way his hair was graying at the temples, snowflakes covering his black strands.

"Let me park my car and I'll walk you across."

"Really, you don't have to do that. I'm fine. Thank you for stopping. Goodnight," she said as she carefully walked across the road as calmly as possible to ensure she didn't do the slip-sliding thing again.

When she opened the door to her home, she entered to hear Charlie talking ten to the dozen with Mrs. Sweet. She smiled as she took her coat and hat off, hanging them over the banister to the stairs, along with her scarf and bag.

"I'm home," she shouted as she walked down the corridor into the kitchen.

"Aunty Tally!" The little boy ran into her arms. She smiled at the nickname he used for her. When he was learning to talk he couldn't pronounce her name so he started calling her Tally and it stuck.

"Hey, my little munchkin. How are you?"

"I'm okay. Mrs. Sweet says I have to go to bed, but

I wanted to wait for you."

"I'm glad you waited," she said, hugging him.

"I told Mrs. Sweet that's what you'd say," Charlie said, looking pleased with himself.

"You know you've got to do what's asked of you."She said

"Yes, and I would have had you not come through the door at that very second," he said in the innocence of a child.

Talia couldn't help but chuckle.

"Far too intelligent for a five-year-old," Mrs. Sweet said as she put her coat on and wrapped a scarf around her neck.

"Umm, you've never said a truer word, Mrs. S." She let Charlie go and stood up to hug the woman who had been her lifesaver. "Thank you for being here with him and all you do for us."

"Don't be silly," Mrs. Sweet said as she hugged her back reassuringly. "I love helping you."

Talia picked up Mrs. Sweet's coat and helped her to slip it on, then walked her to the door. The snow was falling even heavier than before.

"I'll watch you," she said to the sweet, old lady.

Mrs. S went out into the cold and scurried next door, then waved to Talia before she went inside.

Shutting the door, Talia locked and bolted it. Turning around, she saw Charlie sitting on the stairs, his hair still damp from his bath. He was holding onto Alfie, his scruffy teddy bear, which he had when Talia picked him up from the babysitter's, where he had been on the night of the accident.

Her heart ached for him. This little boy had lost everything, his mum, his grandparents, and now he lived with her. They'd had to get to know each other, which terrified her. She'd always been so absorbed in her work that she had never had the time to visit, and if truth be told, she hadn't wanted to. Mum and Dad had always been interested in only Tilly. Her sister had been their pride and joy, although Talia had no doubt her parents had been proud of her.

She took hold of Charlie's hand. "Come on, munchkin, let's get you to bed."

She enclosed his tiny little hand inside hers as they climbed the stairs. They walked into the small bedroom. Toys that he'd been playing with earlier were scattered The Power Ranger figurines matched his pajamas and the posters on the walls around his room.

"Can I have a story?" he asked, looking up at her expectantly, his eyes bright with excitement.

"Of course you can, my love." Her heart filled with tenderness for the little boy who relied on her for everything. Talia had no trouble falling in love with her nephew; there was nothing she wouldn't do for him.

He climbed into bed, and she tucked the duvet around him. Sitting down on the bed, she went to pick up the book they had been reading.

"I've finished reading that one," he said, handing her book two in the series of Enid Blyton's Magical Faraway Stories.

She wasn't surprised. Charlie had the reading ability of a seven-or-eight-year-old, or so April had told her. April had informed her that Charlie was above average in intelligence. Talia was happy that her friend was his teacher. It made her feel secure knowing that she was watching out for him. Just then, Miss Molly jumped onto the duvet to curl up in her usual place at the bottom of his bed.

"Okay," Talia said, taking the book from him. "The Magic Faraway Tree, it is."

She curled up beside him to read the chosen book. Charlie turned on his side toward her and listened to her intently. How could anyone not love him? How could her sister abandon him for weeks at a time with their parents for the sake of another boyfriend?

Tilly always thought of herself first.

* * * *

Max cursed as he tried phoning the car company again, but for some reason, he had no signal, regardless of where he stood. The snow was falling thick and fast now, and it was cold enough to freeze the balls off a brass monkey or even his own! There was no traffic, no one about, and he felt like he was in the middle of nowhere. It seemed that everyone had gone into hibernation as soon as the snow started to fall.

He got back into the car again and tried starting it…zilch! He'd looked under the hood, and there was oil everywhere. He thought it might be a broken oil seal, but he wasn't sure without getting his hands dirty, and that wasn't going to happen at the moment.

Max had to get indoors quick because the snow was coming down fast. The news on the radio had said it was the worst snowfall the UK had in years. Great, it would have to happen while he was there.

Opening the door, he stepped out of the car and shut the door, taking his briefcase with him. Looking at his phone, Max frowned. It was almost out of charge as well. He stepped onto the sidewalk and started walking toward the hotel, then stopped. The girl from the hotel was nearer and she'd have a phone he could use, so he turned around, carefully walking the other way.

Max hadn't seen her since she slipped and fell in the street, but his hours had been crazy, and one night he hadn't even left work and had stayed at his desk. The days had passed into a week, and he'd finally gotten ahead of the problem he had been trying to solve.

The wind started to howl through the trees and he drew up his collar. Obviously, this storm was going to get a lot worse before it got better.

It was further than he'd remembered as he turned into the gateway. He walked down the small driveway where there were two houses side by side. Trees hid the houses; you wouldn't have known they were there.

Which one? There was a car sitting at the side of one of them, but he thought that the car wasn't hers if she was using the bus. So he went to the door of the other house and knocked. *Fuck, it's cold!* He waited and was about to knock again when an outside light came on and the door opened.

"Yes?" An older woman opened the door a crack, just enough for him to see her. Nope, this wasn't her. He was going to sound like some sort of idiot.

"Evening, ma'am." He cleared his throat. "This is going to sound very odd, but I'm looking for the woman who works at The Chester Grosvenor. Talia Wolf."

"You're right, it is very odd. Who are you?" she asked, her tone protective.

"My name is Max Harvey, ma'am. I'm visiting from the United States, working at the Hawarden airplane factory. I'm an aerospace engineer."

"So what do you want with Talia?"

"My car broke down, and she's the only person I know in this area that might be able to help me."

"You haven't got a mobile?" she asked.

"Yes, but there is no signal."

She didn't speak for a moment, and it seemed she was trying to make a judgment.

"The signals are down on the landline phones too…hold on a moment," she said, closing the door.

He stood on the doorstep, absolutely freezing. Stamping his feet, he rubbed his hands together, trying to stay warm. What the *fuck* was he doing? Jesus, he couldn't even feel his fingers or toes. How could it have gotten so cold so quickly? But then again, he had been sitting inside a car with a very nice heater.

The small woman stepped out wrapped in a coat and scarf, with a hat over her gray hair. "Follow me," she said, not even looking at him.

He did as asked, standing behind her as she knocked on the house door a few feet from hers. An outside light lighted up the back, there was a peephole and he assumed she looked through it because it was a few seconds before the door opened. Talia, the woman from the hotel, smiled.

"Mrs. Sweet." She frowned when she saw him. "Come in." She stood aside for them to enter.

"No, I won't, I came over with this gentleman who says he knows you and I wanted to make sure before I let him near you."

He wanted to laugh. How would she have managed to stop him? Perhaps she had witching powers and would have turned him into a mouse. She turned to look at him as if knowing exactly what he was thinking…now that was scary.

"You are from the Grosvenor," she said rather than asked.

He nodded.

"How can I help you?" Talia asked him, frowning.

Before he had a chance to answer, the old lady intervened. "So, are you all right with this? It's too cold for me out here. I just want to get back to my kitty and coal fire."

Talia looked at him for a moment and narrowed her eyes. "Yes, Mrs. Sweet. You get back in before you freeze."

"You know where I am if you need anything," she said over her shoulder as she walked carefully back to her home.

"What can I do for you, Mr. Harvey?"

He noticed that worried frown appeared again, but what did he expect? She didn't know him from Adam, and he knew that his appearance of six and a half feet was somewhat daunting to most people.

"Max," he said.

She hesitated for a moment before she opened the door wider. "Come in and get warm by the fire."

She stood aside for him to enter, and he didn't need to asked twice. His whole body was numb from the cold, and he felt like he would never thaw out.

He stamped his feet on the mat as he came in and unbuttoned his coat before slipping it off. She took it from him. "It should dry here as it's next to the radiator. Come through," she said, and he followed her down a narrow hallway.

The room they entered had a fire with logs blazing in the grate. Max went to stand in front of it. Within seconds, he could feel the warmth penetrate his clothes, and he let his hands hover over the heat for a moment before turning around.

Talia stood a little anxious by the door. She had on a loose sweater and a pair of slim jeans. Her short bangs were disheveled as if she'd been pushing her fingers through it. He thought she looked troubled

"So, what is the problem?" she asked him.

He explained to her what had happened, and she listened intently. She pursed her lips as if thinking about what to do.

"The phone lines are down, not even the mobiles are working," she said.

"Yeah, I know. I can't get any cell coverage."

"The weather doesn't seem to be getting any better. I don't think I've seen it this bad for a very long time," Talia spoke as she moved from the door to the window and pushed aside the curtain to look outside.

Max went to stand beside her, and his heart sank. The falling snow completely covered the ground, it was not letting up. And now the wind had started to blow. It was a blizzard condition.

He turned his attention back to her. She stood with her arms folded, and this close he saw a weariness in her face and tiredness that seemed to seep from her.

"Looks like I'm in your hands," he said. "I know this must seem creepy to you, but I didn't know anyone else and you were close by."

"We hardly know each other," she said. "Bumping into each other in the corridor doesn't constitute us being friends."

"I know, and I'm sorry to put this on you, but it looks like I need somewhere to stay, at least until the snow stops and the phone lines are repaired. I will, of course, pay you for the inconvenience."

"I don't have a spare room," she said.

"The sofa will do," he said, looking at the small two-seater and wondering how his enormous frame would fit. He dragged his hand over the back of his neck, feeling the pain just by looking.

He looked back at her, and she had her fingers over her mouth, suppressing a grin. Her entire face lit up, and behind those enormous glasses, her eyes sparkled. He felt his heart somersault, not just once but in quick succession, steadily increasing his heart rate. Was it healthy to feel like this after seeing someone a few times? He was an adult man, not a teenager, but that was how she made him feel.

Hmm…

* * * *

Talia must have been insane, but what could she do? She flipped the switch up on the kettle to make some tea. Taking off her glasses, she rubbed at her eyes, pinching the bridge of her nose. The flickers of bright spots dancing in front of her eyes, her vision momentarily blinded by anxiety, surprised her. But there was something about him that suggested trust, and her instincts were usually good.

He was good-looking, which was strange for her to notice because she never did. He spoke calmly in a low voice. It was hard not to recognize his American accent, and it could have easily lulled her into a mesmeric state of awe. Jesus, she must be more tired than she thought.

Talia leaned back wearily against the kitchen countertop. She was exhausted. The night before she hadn't gotten hardly any sleep because Charlie had a nightmare, which was unusual for him. She could only think it was because of the time of year, poor little guy.

Talia's mind wandered to the strange man in her

living room. Even though it was almost eleven at night and the guy looked as if he'd had a truck full of snow over him, he was a handsome, well-dressed man. She'd seen that when they'd bumped into each other twice in the hotel.

She wasn't exactly attractive, especially in her holey, well-worn jeans and a comfortably oversized sweater that was made for warmth rather than meeting someone from where she worked, particularly a man who looked like he should be in the boardroom than her living room.

Ah, well! She sighed.

One minute she'd been up to her knees on a dig in Greece and the next day she'd become an adopted mum and her sister's primary carer. In theory, Talia had lost her family in a split second. It didn't matter how dysfunctional her family was.It hurt like hell when she received the phone call about the accident.

Her flight from Greece had felt like the longest ever. She had been in a daze when April had met her at Manchester Airport. At that point, she'd been running on invisible energy. She suddenly realized what she was returning home to when she saw her friend's tear-stained face. Even now a lump settled in her throat.

Meow.

Putting her glasses back on, she looked down at Molly, the stray cat Charlie had found in the garden a few weeks ago. He had pleaded with Talia to keep the somewhat straggly cat, who looked like it hadn't eaten for a while. Since then Charlie had named her and loved her like, she was his own. Talia had posted flyers describing the cat, but no one had come forward.

Talia had never had a cat. She traveled around and

an animal would not have been conducive to her arrangements. She opened the cupboard and took out two mugs, popping in a tea bag.

Meow. The cat wrapped herself around Talia's ankles.

"Okay, I'm going to get some milk now," she said to Molly as she opened the fridge, taking out the container. "Here you go," she said as she went over to the cat's dish, bent down, and poured some out. Talia stood up, watching the cat lift up the liquid as if she'd never seen it.

"Is there anything I can do to help?"

Talia looked up and almost dropped the milk. "Goodness, you startled me," she said more breathlessly than she needed to.

Max offered her a smile. He looked tired as he rubbed his fingers through his short beard.

"Sorry, I didn't mean to," he said, the genuine concern in his eyes surprising her a little, because she liked the look. It felt good to have someone care about her, even if it was just for a few seconds. The last year had been lonely and exhausting. There had been no time for her to think about having her own life.

"Tea is nearly made," she said, turning around and pouring the water from the boiling kettle into the cups. "Milk?" she asked.

"Yes, please."

She poured milk into both cups, picked them up, and set them on the kitchen table.

"Please, sit down. Help yourself to sugar," Talia said as she pushed the bowl on the table toward him.

He looked so flipping big standing in her small doorway that she was glad when he pulled a chair out to sit down. He'd taken off his coat and suit jacket. His white shirt was stark against the tanned skin, and she could see a few strands of dark hair peeping out at the neck with two buttons open. He was what her friend would determine as *hot*.

April tried to set her up on various dates whenever Talia came home. It was so embarrassing, but she had to confess; it amused her. She often told April she should have been a wedding planner rather than a teacher.

Talia never felt bored or lonely when she worked on unique sights in exceptional countries. She had to admit that since leaving her work in Greece, it was only then that she realized how much it had meant to her.

"So, what brings you to Chester?" she asked as she picked up her cup and blew the steam from her tea before taking a sip.

"Work, I'm an aerospace engineer," he said as a smile creased his face.

"I don't know what I expected, but it wasn't that." She smiled.

"I don't know whether to be offended or not." Max chuckled.

She was quick to defend her assumption. "It's just not what I was expecting. So, what brings you here?"

"I'm doing some work at the Hawarden airplane factory. My designs are a little tricky and need some adjusting."

He smiled as he leaned forward, putting his elbows on the tabletop as his hands surrounded the mug of tea, and her eyes were immediately stuck on how big they were. He had beautifully shaped fingers for a man, and she couldn't help but think of how they would feel on her skin. *Bloody hell.*

"Designs?" she asked.

"Yes, they are proving to be a little more intricate than I had initially thought."

"Wow, that must be interesting."

"I think so," he said, giving her a very sexy, alluring, desirous smile, which was probably in her mind only.

Talia took a large swig of tea. It was too much and as she swallowed, she nearly choked. *Oh God.* She coughed until she thought she would never breathe normally again, and it didn't help that Max had gotten up from his chair and gently rubbed her back.

"Let me get you a glass of water," he said as he took one from the drainer and filled it from the tap. He handed it to her, and Talia carefully sipped it slowly.

"Thank you."

"Okay?" He was leaning down, looking at her with concern in his eyes.

"Yes, yes, I'm fine…sorry about that."

When he continued to look at her she blushed even more. Even though a shiver shimmied down her spine and back again, Talia was sure her temperature was well over a hundred.

"Really," she said. "Please sit down and finish your tea."

For a second he stood there before going back to his chair.

Good grief, she needed to give herself a stern talking-to. She had no idea what on earth was going on with her. Talia was the sensible one, the plain one, and she never thought about a man as she was thinking about this one.

"So, have you traveled from America or do you already live in the UK?" she said, trying to break the connection that seemed to be prevalent between them.

"I live in Washington DC," he said without taking his eyes from hers.

"Will you go home for Christmas?"

"I'm hoping to, even if it means I must return afterward."

"I'm sure your family will miss you if you don't," Talia said as she managed to look down at her tea instead of staring at him. But when she looked back up it was to find his eyes still on her in a way that wasn't just conversational…there was something else there, but she couldn't figure out what it was.

He smiled, and she thought she could detect a hint of sadness in those eyes. "I have no family, but I'm lucky to have good friends who put up with me at this time of year."

"Oh, I'm sorry," she murmured, realizing that she was practically in the same position, but at least she still had Charlie and she could visit with her sister. "Right," Talia announced , standing up. "Let me get you some bedding."

He pushed his chair back and followed her into the living room.

She put some more logs on the fire and turned around. "Please feel free to keep topping up the fire through the night," she said as she shoved her hands into her back pockets. He was way too tall for this room; his long legs would be hanging over the end of the sofa.

"Thank you, Talia. I am so grateful to you. I didn't fancy spending the night in my car."

"No problem. Let's hope the phones will be accessible soon. Even the mobile phone signal is still down."

He nodded, and they stood looking at each other for a moment before she cleared her throat.

"Okay, I'll go get that bedding." She brushed past him, quickly exiting the room.

Bloody hell.

Chapter 3

Max groaned as he opened his eyes. His back was as stiff as a board, and he had no feeling in his feet at all. But the dream he'd been having made him ravenous for the woman he'd only just met, and that never happened to him. He experienced lust like any typical male, but a need so powerful that he dreamed about it... No, never before.

He imagined her close, her lips on his jaw and nuzzling his neck. It was insane but he was so painfully aroused it hurt like hell. He closed his eyes for a moment, trying not to think about her in that way.

His hand encountered something furry, and he opened his eyes immediately to see a black cat with an annoying bell sitting on his chest, staring back at him. After the initial shock, he stroked the silky fur down its back. "Hello there, and who might you be?"

"Her name is Molly," came a small voice behind him.

Was that a child's voice?

Max turned his head toward the voice, moving quicker than he should have since his neck felt like it didn't belong to him. He was right, damn, it was a little boy in blue pajamas, carrying a teddy under one arm. He had short, light blond hair and the deepest dark brown eyes framed by long, dark lashes.

The cat had jumped off him and he swung his legs

to the floor, keeping the duvet tucked around him as he only had his boxers on.

"Hello," he said. "I'm Max."

"I know, Aunty Tally told me. My name is Charlie. I'm not supposed to come in here so as not to wake you, but Molly ran off and I was trying to stop her from jumping on you."

"It's nice to meet you, Charlie."

"Are you staying for breakfast?"

He laughed. There was nothing like a child's natural inquisition.

"Charlie," a voice from behind the boy said. "Leave Mr. Harvey alone." The fixation of his dreams walked through the door wearing a pair of jeans and a black turtleneck. She had her hair pulled back loosely, and those large glasses rested atop her slender nose.

The little boy turned. "Can I have pancakes for breakfast?" he asked Talia.

"Of course you can, but you must get dressed first."

"Okay," he said in a reluctant voice as he walked away.

"And Charlie."

"Yeah," he said as he stopped to look over his shoulder.

"Clean your teeth."

"Really? I did them last night, they don't need to be cleaned again," he said in a tone that made Max want to laugh out loud, but of course, he didn't.

"Charlie, why do we have this discussion every morning?"

"Because it's silly to clean them in the morning."

"Do you know what is silly?" Talia asked him.

"What?"

"That you even think you're going to win this debate."

"Huh, doesn't seem fair that you win all the time, Aunty Tally…it isn't." And with his shoulders slumped he walked away with what seemed the world on his shoulders.

As soon as he was gone, Talia turned to Max with a grin on her face. "That boy is way too old for a nearly six-year-old," she said, and it was pretty clear to him that she wanted to laugh.

They both stared at each other, her soul-searching eyes not helping the affliction denting his boxers.

She cleared her throat. "Right, I'll leave you to get dressed. Tea or coffee?" she asked.

"Coffee is great, thanks."

"I only have instant."

"That's good."

She pushed her glasses back up her nose and stared at him for a few seconds before turning around and leaving the room, shutting the door behind her.

He sighed as he leaned back on the sofa. Given the heat of his interest, he didn't need the duvet to cover him. Throwing back the cover, he reached for his pants. He shivered at the cold. The fire had gone out, with only a smidgen of glowing embers left.

Shrugging into his shirt, he hastily fastened the buttons and slipped on his pants before reaching around to pull back the curtains. He couldn't believe what he saw. The snow was at least three feet deep, still coming down in large, crystal-like flakes. The sky was so dark it was hard to imagine it was morning and not night.

Slipping his hand into his trouser pocket, he pulled out his phone and switched it on. Setting it on the coffee table to give it a moment to connect, he moved aside the fire guard and carefully selected some firewood from the bucket along with some coal. And emptied it on the burning embers and waited for it to catch before moving the guard back in front of the fire.

His heart sank when he picked up his phone and saw no service. The connections must still be out, and judging by the amount of snow that had fallen overnight and was still falling, it looked like he would be there for a while. At least he'd had the foresight to bring his briefcase with him, which meant he could do some work.

He was generally a light sleeper and could survive on four hours a night, but when he looked at his watch and saw that it was 8:15 AM, he was slightly surprised. Mind you, given the erotic dream he'd been having he wished he was still sleeping.

A helluva way to start the day

* * * *

Talia put some bread in the toaster and leaned against the counter, crossing her arms over her chest. Her stomach fluttered as her thoughts drifted to the man in her living room. What exactly was it that she found appealing about this man? She pursed her lips as she considered the question. He had a fan of dark lashes that she would die for, his almond-shaped eyes were dark and seductive, and his full lips covered straight, white teeth. But most of all she liked his beard, the way it shadowed his square jaw, not too short but not too long.

Talia chuckled to herself. Men had never been a priority in her life. She was more interested in the bronze age, and the Minoan civilization turned her on more than men could. She had spent the last twelve years of her life studying, getting her doctorate at the University of

Manchester, and studying digs on the island of Crete in Greece.

She'd given it all up to come home and look after her nephew. Talia missed her old life, but she didn't regret returning for the little boy sitting at the table eating his Coco Pops, milk dripping down his chin. She was about to wipe it away with some tissue when he used his sleeve. *Yep, that would do it.* She laughed to herself.

It wasn't long before her mind wandered again to the man getting dressed, and she tried to figure out his appeal. It could have been the well-maintained body. He had more than attractive muscles to any female, but even she wasn't that naive not to realize that. For goodness' sake, she had felt them twice and had acted unconsciously to protect herself.

Max made her feel things she'd never felt before. Of course she'd had sex, but that's all it had ever been, and to be honest she found her work more interesting. Shaking her head, she wondered what on earth had gotten into her. Men were not part of her life. She had enough to do keeping her and Charlie safe from his lunatic father.

The thought of Roy made her shudder. She'd managed to keep on the move; hopefully, he had lost interest by now. Spending a few months in one spot had felt good, and it had been necessary for Charlie's feeling of belonging. The poor little guy had been all over the place. But Chester had been her home, and she'd felt good staying here.

"Aunty Tally, smoke, smoke. The toast is burning."

The fire alarm brought her abruptly out of her thoughts, and she quickly disconnected the toaster.

Blasted thing!

The screech of the alarm made her want to bash it with something hard, but before she had a chance to do that it turned off. Max had come into the kitchen and reached up to shut the noise off.

"Aunty Tally burnt the toast again," her delightful nephew spurted out as he pushed away his empty dish.

"Thank you, Charlie, for that little snippet of information," Talia said.

"You're always telling me that the truth is important."

Why was it that he had a ten-year-olds intelligence but six-year-olds tantrums?

"Yes, I do, and you did," she said tongue in cheek at being told off by this miniature person.

Talia looked at Max to see a definite smile twitching at the corners of his mouth, and she smiled at him. Charlie was right, she did the same thing every morning.

Talia made a concerted effort to focus on what she was doing. She had always been prone to effortlessly slipping into another reality. Usually, she would have been working on that project.

She turned her attention to the man standing in her tiny kitchen. "Thanks for turning that off. I normally have to get a chair to reach it."

"No problem. I'm glad to be of some use."

"I thought we were having pancakes?" Charlie asked, his little lips pursed into what she knew could become a tantrum.

"We were, but I forgot to get eggs. As soon as it stops snowing I'll get some and make you some chocolate chip ones."

She hoped that would deter him from making a fuss. Thankfully, it worked.

"Sit down please," she said to Max. "How do you take your coffee?"

"Black, no sugar please."

"You can sit next to me if you like," Charlie said.

"Thank you, I'd like that," Max said as he drew out the chair and sat down.

"But if you are expecting any toast like I was, I don't think you're going to get any, because when Aunty Tally burns it we have to let the toaster cool down for a while."

"Thank you, Charlie, for stating the obvious," Talia said.

"It might be obvious to me, but Max might not know it."

Talia put a mug of coffee next to Max and corrected Charlie, "Mr. Harvey."

"He said I could call him Max, didn't you?" He turned his face to look up at the man sitting next to him.

"Indeed I did, Charlie."

A hum of pleasure reached his chubby, little face as it smiled at her. Hmm, she saw how this was.

"Huh, two against one, is it?" she murmured as she took his dish and put it into the sink for washing.

Max chuckled. "Certainly not." But the lift of his eyebrow told her differently.

She sat down with her tea and looked out of the kitchen window, but all you could see was white. "Seems like the snow is not letting up, and still no phone lines. Thankfully, the power is still on, although it has flickered twice this morning."

"Yeah, I'm just trying to decide what to do."

"Well, I can tell you that because we are not accustomed to this type of weather, the services will not have made preparations. You'll probably stay inside until the snow stops until then.

"Aww, does that mean no Christmas tree today?" Charlie asked, the disappointment in his face as clear as daylight.

"I'm afraid so," she said as she ruffled his hair.

His face dropped to the floor, and she hated to see him looking so sad and disappointed.

"But it means we can make a snowman later on if you'd like to?"

Immediately, a smile split his face into the most beautiful delight. "We can?"

She nodded. "But first you need to make your bed and tidy your clothes away from yesterday."

He jumped from his chair and shot out of the kitchen as if the roadrunner was after him.

Talia laughed out loud but stopped when she saw Max looking at her.

"I can't remember such enthusiasm at that age to clean my room." He chuckled.

"Don't be fooled, he has his agenda and that's playing in the snow."

"Even so…"

"Because I work, we have to be organized, and Charlie is very untidy, and also, he has to learn to clean up after himself."

"I agree," he said.

Why did she feel the need to enlighten the man sitting across from her?

"You don't have to explain your actions to me," he said as he cradled his cup.

Every single cell tingled at the sound of his voice. It was so deep and gravelly that she could become mesmerized by the sound of him speaking.

Was that normal?

She wished she could phone April because it was certainly not something she'd ever experienced. She hardly knew the guy, but every man she had known, not one of them had made her feel like she wanted to be ravished at that very moment.

The poor man hadn't asked to be there, it was circumstances that no one had foreseen. Since they collided in the hotel hallway, he had probably forgotten all about her, and why would he? One thing Talia knew, she wasn't as stunning as her sister Tilly.

She looked at Max to find him staring at her, and he raised his eyebrows.

"You were deep in thought?"

She smiled. "Not really. I was thinking that being away from home at this time of year must be tough. Do you have children?" A perfectly normal question, although her reasons weren't.

"No, I'm not married and have no children."

Why did her heart do the waltz? She chose to ignore it, although her hormones wouldn't oblige.

"Judging by the amount of snow that has fallen, and is still coming down, it looks like you might be stuck here today," she said as they both stared out the window.

"I have my laptop so I can work with it. Are you sure you don't mind me staying? I could walk and see if I can find a taxi?"

"No way is there going to be any traffic on the road today. In the UK, we only have to have a dusting of flakes and the whole country goes into meltdown," she said, laughing.

"It's very kind of you to let me stay."

"Think of it as my good deed for the season"

She had a thought, but she wasn't sure how he would react.

"I don't suppose you would like to come outside with us and make a snowman?"

He looked surprised, and she thought she saw an uncomfortable expression in his eyes. Of course he wasn't interested. He was a sexy, successful guy. Men like him didn't hang out with single ladies who had a child.

Heat decided to crawl up her cheeks, and she was sure—in fact, she was one hundred and ten percent sure—that she was blushing.

"Never mind," she said before he had a chance to reply. "It was only a suggestion, but you must have work to do." She got up and took both their cups to the sink. "Can I make you some toast now that the toaster has cooled down?"

Talia turned around to find him looking at her. She felt her hormones do somersaults, and she wanted to stop staring at the man, but she couldn't.

"I would like to come outside and help build a snowman, but I'm not sure how good I would be as it's something I've never done."

She narrowed her eyes, unsure what to make of his statement. Was he just being polite? "You've never made a snowman?"

"No."

"Holy cow." She was astonished. "Why?"

"Why what?" he asked.

"Why do you want to come outside into the freezing cold?"

He smiled, and it was a kind, sincere, sexy smile.

"Because you asked so nicely, and it sounds like

fun."

"I'm not sure about fun, but it will be cold, and Charlie will love it."

"I'd better have some toast then, keep my energy up," he said, amusement in his eyes.

"Brace yourself, because you'll either hate it or love it."

* * * *

Max didn't know what he'd let himself in for, but it sounded fun and it looked like he'd have plenty of time to work later. The snow wasn't letting up anytime soon. He stood at the kitchen window, waiting for Charlie and Talia, and all he could see was whiteness. It was coming down heavily. Talia had gone to see if Mrs. Sweet had any of her son's wellingtons for him to wear. Max laughed as he looked at his expensive, size twelve, Italian leather shoes.

Even the heating on it made him shiver to see the overcast sky. He could almost feel the coldness go right through him to his bones. It wasn't the first time he'd seen snow. When he went to the cabin with his friends Jarrod and Liam in winter, it was to enjoy the skiing. But somehow it wasn't the same. He guessed they didn't notice the cold so much up there.

Max figured it would be fun to make a snowman, perhaps a childhood re-spent at one of the things he'd never done. He and his two friends had met in the system, all parentless, and they'd been shuffled into children's homes, because no one wanted them. It hadn't been easy, but he knew it would have been far harder if he'd been on his own.

Unlike Jarrod and Liam, his mom had died giving birth to him. It had been just his dad and himself until he was fourteen. His dad had been very much like a mad scientist, but he couldn't imagine a life without him, never thought he would have to.

It had been an exciting childhood. Though not particularly successful, Max's father had invented many items. He also worked as a grocery store employee, and loved it because it allowed him to interact with and assist customers.

Although his dad was a simple guy, he was also a genius, and some of his designs were brilliant. When Max was older and had gone sifting through some of the designs his father had left, he understood.

He could still vividly recall the shock he had experienced upon learning that his father was shot during a robbery at the bank where he had been depositing his paycheck.

He'd had no family, no one else to look after him, and with only two boxes to his name he'd been sent to a children's home. He still missed the craziness that had been his dad. Max suddenly had an overwhelming feeling of loneliness. He had no wife, no children, and no real home.

The very tidy, masculine apartment he had in Georgetown overlooking the Potomac River was just somewhere to hang his hat and work. Most times he worked from his home office unless he had to go on-site like now to continue his job.

Talia was not the usual type of woman that caught his attention. He drew his eyebrows together as he wondered what it was about her that he couldn't quite put his finger on. She wasn't obviously beautiful, but there was an underlying loveliness, even though she tried to hide it with those awful, big glasses.

What was her story? Why was she looking after her nephew? Before he had time to consider it further a voice brought him out of his thoughts.

"Can ya help me with my wellies?"

What were wellies?

He turned around to look at the boy. Charlie had his coat on, buttoned up wrong, and his red and white hat was half-on and half-off. He was sitting on the floor, trying to pull his wellingtons on, which were as red as his chubby cheeks.

"Sure," Max said as he went on his haunches, trying not to laugh at the unexpected dishevelment that was looking up at him. "So, these are your wellies," he said, more in an understanding of the word than an answer.

"Yeah. Aunty Tally bought them for me."

"Lucky boy."

Charlie nodded his head vigorously.

"There you go," Max said, and the little boy stood up. Max automatically straightened his hat. "Do you have gloves and a scarf?"

While pulling his gloves out of his coat pocket and wriggling them in front of Max, Charlie nodded vehemently. But I can't seem to find my scarf anywhere.

"Umm, I wonder if Aunty Tally might know where it is?"

"She will, she knows everything."

Max chuckled.

"Here you go, Charlie, put your scarf on too. I hope you're not bothering Max."

"No, I only asked for his help." He turned back to Max. "You didn't mind, did ya?"

"Of course I didn't." He couldn't help but smile at the sweet boy.

"Yes, well, thousands would believe you, but I know Charlie," she said as she wrapped the fluffy scarf around his neck. "He can talk for England."

"What does that mean, Aunty Tally?" The little boy frowned up at Talia.

She smiled at him, it was a smile full of love as her hand cupped his chubby cheek. "It means you talk a lot."

"Is that okay?" He pushed out his lip a little and Talia went on her knees, hugging him hard before leaning back to cup his cheeks.

"Of course it is, honey. I wouldn't have you any other way." And she gave him a big kiss on the lips.

"Aww, Aunty Tally, that was wet and sloppy," he said, brushing the back of his hand across his lips.

She laughed. "The best kind," she said before getting up.

As Max watched the happiness and love that flowed from one to the other it made his chest constrict. He'd forgotten what that kind of love was like. It had been so long since he'd felt anything like that. Max was lying to himself, because Maisy, his friend Jarrod's wife, was very loving.

He remembered the first time he'd met Maisy. She'd immediately hugged him, which was one of those hugs full of love. He figured Jarrod had told her about their upbringing, but it wasn't a sympathetic love. Considering what she had been through, she still saw the best in everyone. He did not doubt that she would make a great mom again, when her baby came, which was going to be very soon.

In an instant, he saw sadness in Talia's eyes. For a moment, he focused his on hers until she shifted her gaze and he wondered if it may have been his imagination. His interest in her was more than just sexual, although their chemistry was off the charts.

"Wellies from Mrs. Sweet." Talia held them up for him to see, then set them in front of him. "They should fit, because her son is nearly as tall as you. And I've brought some other things for you too." She handed him the items in her arms—a thick jacket, scarf, and other clothes. "I'm guessing you're going to get wet, so there are some clothes for you to change once you come back in."

Her cheeks were flushed as she stood in front of him, her green woolly hat covering her hair, the matching scarf wrapped a few times around her neck. She looked like a little girl. Her eyes were sparkling behind her large glasses. He'd love to take them off and kiss each eye.

It was time he let the snow freeze his libido before it got him into trouble.

"That's great, thank you," he said, and was ready in a few minutes.

"Come on, Max." And just like that, Charlie's little hand went into his, and the strangest feeling squeezed at his heart.

* * * *

Talia breathed in the cold air. It was welcoming, because although it was freezing she was decidedly warm. She was too young for menopause and didn't think she was sick. The only other explanation she could think of for the heat wave she was experiencing was the man who was helping them build a snowman.

Although her sister was still alive, the court had made Talia a legal guardian of her nephew. Then Tilly's ex-husband appeared, demanding she hand over his son. That was not going to happen, and the court agreed that

Roy was an unfit parent because of his record as a drug dealer and heroin addict. He was a nasty piece of work. She had no idea what her sister had thought when she married him. Within six months they had been divorced.

Talia had a restraining order on him, because he wouldn't leave them alone, and quite frankly, she was terrified of him. But he pursued them as they moved from one place to another. When they were safe, she hadn't seen any signs of him…but for how long?

Her heart constricted as she looked at the little boy who was having so much fun. This child never complained. She loved him so much. Talia never considered Tilly's son until she was informed of the accident and returned home. She had only ever seen him when she had returned home.

Sometimes when she was on a dig she'd be there for months and months, not even taking a break as she loved her work so much. Her life now was so different to what it had been. She'd never been responsible for anyone but herself, but it hadn't taken her long to feel very protective of Charlie. He was so easy to love.

Leaving a job she loved had been hard, but a dig was no place for a child. With her doctorate degree, she could have lectured at any university. But because of Charlie's dad, they had been unable to settle down, and so working in hotels seemed like the best option. Her savings had quickly dwindled with the extra money she had to pay for Tilley's care.

She was so deep in thought that when a snowball came her way she nearly jumped out of her skin. Looking around, she spotted the culprit. He had the cheekiest, cutest grin ever and jumped up and down in excitement.

She narrowed her eyes, bent down to gather some

snow, and rolled it about in her hands. "Okay, you little rascal, you better be afraid."

His giggle was infectious, and she caught Max's eye. There was a mischievous look on his face as he went on his haunches to help the little boy gather up some snow.

Talia couldn't help the laughter that emitted from her as she threw a snowball before they could make another one.

"Come on, Charlie, don't let her escape."

Talia was laughing so much that she couldn't run and a giant snowball came in her direction. She ducked just in time to miss it, but she slipped, falling to the ground.

"We got you, we got you." Charlie jumped on her, screaming with joy.

"You cheated," she said, giggling like a teenager. "Two against one is so unfair."

"No, it wasn't," Max said, looking down at her. "You are bigger than Charlie." He had one heck of a teasing glint in his eye, and Talia didn't know where it came from, but she grabbed at his booted leg and knocked him off balance.

Charlie was laughing beside himself, and he got up to sit on Max. But the big man she'd knocked over didn't move. After a moment, she started to panic. *Oh shit, he's not moving.* Scrambling to her feet, she leaned over him.

Before she could say his name, however, she was pulled down and found Talia lying by his side.

"Hahaha, Max got you, hahaha." Charlie laughed so hard.

"You monster," Talia said, laughing at Max, looking at his face.

Then suddenly, neither of them was laughing as Charlie got up to roll around in the snow.

"Are you okay?" Max asked her as he turned on his side.

"Yes, are you?" she asked as she turned to face him.

"Uh-huh."

Their breath swirled in front of them, and she was so close she could feel the warmth of his on her lips.

He reached up and pushed the hair from her forehead before drawing her glasses off. "You have amazing eyes, like bowls of caramel with bits of chocolate in them."

"I do?"

"Yes."

"Thank you." She didn't know what else to say. No one had ever said that about her.

"Look out, look out, here I come." Charlie jumped on both of them and the spell between them broke. But for the first time in her life, in those fleeting seconds, she started to think of a man as a man rather than just a colleague.

Chapter 4

Max enjoyed the heat of the water as the shower powered out. He used the body wash he'd received and lathered it up through his hair and body. The hot water ran down his body, rinsing away the gel, and he stood with his head down, allowing the warmth to soak into his tense muscles.

Talia had such an innocence about her, which was very striking, but her inner beauty shined through and it was that which he found so attractive. She had an effect on his emotions that he didn't understand, but he did recognize the excitement in the pit of his stomach.

But he felt she had a sense of sorrow about her, and several times he'd noticed her looking distant as she'd watched him and Charlie play in the snow. She had an unyielding strength that emitted from her, but he'd also noticed a fear in her eyes, first at the hotel, and again when she thought no one was looking at her.

For the first time in a long time Max wanted to ask someone else what was wrong. Why did she carry that fear in her eyes? His desire to learn more about her shocked him a little. He had never felt like that before about a woman. He told himself he should get out of there now. Nonetheless, he couldn't; not just because of the situation with the weather, but he didn't want to.

And he'd had fun outside. He hadn't thought it would be possible as he'd had no experience with children, but it was very invigorating to hear the small boy's laughter and witness his childlike innocence. Max had been in the snow many times, but only skiing with friends at his cabin in the mountains, never in a woman and child's company before.

Stepping out of the shower, he got dressed in the jeans and sweater Talia had borrowed from Mrs. Sweet. They were a good fit; her son must have a similar physique to his own.

He went downstairs to the kitchen, but there was no sign of either Talia or Charlie. So he went into the living room where he had slept and put another log on the glowing embers in the fireplace. Sitting down, he picked up his briefcase and opened it.

Molly sat beside him, curling up next to his thigh. He stroked the long, black fur and she meowed with pleasure, going on her back so he could tickle her tummy. Max succumbed to her wanting for a few minutes before drawing his laptop out. Setting it on his knee, he flipped the lid open and switched it on.

About an hour later, Max heard voices, and he lifted his head as a bundle of incessant chatter came into the room. Charlie came and sat beside him, stroking Molly.

"We've been to see Mrs. Sweet," Charlie said as he kicked off his wellies, at the same time yanking his hat off, clutching it in his hand. "What are you doing?" he asked Max, but before he could answer, Charlie continued. "I like playing games on there." He pointed to the screen. "But Aunty Tally only lets me on there for half an hour a day. But in school, we get to work on them."

"Charlie, pick up your boots and hang up your things."

"But—"

"But nothing."

Max had no idea why, but the little boy made him want to laugh out loud, but he decided that wouldn't be appropriate. Then Charlie left the room and Talia burst out laughing.

"I shouldn't laugh, but sometimes I can't help it when I see the look on his face." She giggled.

She had surprised him, because he hadn't seen any signs of amusement on her face when she had spoken to the little boy.

"I have no idea how to raise a child, but you seem to be doing a good job," Max said.

A small smile creased her face, and a faint flush tinged her cheeks. "Believe me, it's not something that has come naturally," Talia said as she moved toward the fire, setting the guard aside. She lifted two logs from the bucket to throw them on the glowing redness. Blue hues flickered from the sparks. They both watched it for a moment before she turned around. "I need to go get some more wood."

"I'll do that. It's the least I can do." He set his laptop on the table and stood up.

"You don't have to."

"I know that, but I would like to," he said as they both had a hand on the bucket. Tallia hesitated for a moment before letting go.

"Okay," she said. "It's a job I hate, but I'll cook you some lunch in return."

"It's a deal," he said as he followed behind her, trying to keep his gaze off her adorable ass and not having much luck until she stopped and he almost knocked her over.

"You'll need to wrap up. It's a cold job in this weather. She opened a door beneath the stairs and lifted a large bin out with both hands before he could do it. "I keep a big bin in here," she said. He wondered what a bin was, and then this large, plastic trash can appeared. "If you fill this and then return it here, it keeps the logs dry."

"Okay, that doesn't sound too difficult," he said, picking up the heavy bin. Damn, how did she manage to move this when it was full?

"The logs are in the shed at the bottom of the garden. Transfer some to the fireplace when you come in."

"No problem," he said as he went to put on his outdoor clothes

"Thank you. I'll have a cup ready for you when you come back in."

He opened the door. The snow, which was still falling, was cold, and the air was fresh. Looking up, he saw dark clouds. It didn't look like the weather would clear up anytime soon.

As he stepped outside, he noticed some large footprints. That was strange. They weren't his because the falling snow would have covered them by now. The crunching of his boots against the winter elements sounded loud in the eeriness of the quietly falling flakes.

Something was making the back of his neck prickle, a mechanism he'd picked up from being in the children's home. He narrowed his eyes as he looked around him, but it was getting hard to see beyond what was right in front of him. Geez, they didn't have weather this bad at his cabin in Beech Mountain, North Carolina.

* * * *

Max sat at the table with Talia and Charlie, and she couldn't decide if that was a good or bad thing. Charlie loved having him there, although she wasn't sure how Max felt because her little nephew could talk and talk.

Talia lacked a sizable social network. On the digs

where she worked and while pursuing her doctorate, she made some friends.

April was her best friend, but since she'd married her priorities had changed, which was fine. Talia knew that April would always be on the phone if she needed her.

She watched as Max showed genuine interest in Charlie and what he was saying about his Lego and the spaceship he was trying to build. Talia had wanted to help him but had no idea how to. It was a learning curve, just like everything else she'd had to deal with in the last year.

She picked up the milk and eggs to return them to the refrigerator. Thank goodness Mrs. Sweet had some extra eggs to give her. Talia's lips moved into a smile as she heard Charlie ask Max if he liked Lego. It was strange how he made her feel. She closed the door, and picking up her cup, she sipped the tea as she watched them both.

Max happened to look up then and smiled, making her feel strangely good. She felt her pulse flutter in her throat and put her hand to it as she smiled back at him.

Talia liked how his hair was graying at the temples, and she loved his beard, it was very sexy, and she wanted to know how it felt against her fingers. How ridiculous she was, it was so obscure to think this way, so totally unlike her. Perhaps having Charlie was giving her a different perspective on life.

Max could have retreated to the living room, but he hadn't. *Ask him why he didn't* a tiny voice in her head said. Crap, she just wasn't made that way. Now, if it had been April, her friend, she would have already known his shirt size. Talia wanted to laugh aloud at the idea.

"Shall we take all of this into the living room? It will be warmer in there," she said to the two bent heads.

They used a tray for the Lego pieces to make it easy to move. Charlie looked at Max.

"That's a great idea. Come on, Charlie," Max said as he lifted the tray. "You bring the box."

Her nephew nodded. "This is going to be so good, isn't it, Max?"

Max grinned. "Yeah, bud, it's going to be awesome."

"Awesome," Charlie repeated, and Talia was left to follow them with a smile.

Charlie, Max, and Talia sat by the fire, with Charlie and Max on the floor and Talia attempting to read the pages in front of her from a couch. As she saw him patiently instructing Charlie as they meticulously constructed the spaceship, she felt a flutter in her stomach.

He was very handsome, and it was obvious he worked out. She didn't doubt for one moment that he was short of female adulation. But it was the kindness she saw in his eyes, the softness in his smile when he talked to Charlie, that made her see a man who cared.

His shoes, neatly tucked under the coffee table, were well-made and expensive, just like his suit. Max was friendly, but Talia wasn't sure why his gaze made her heart race.

She turned slightly to look out the bay window. It was such a picturesque scene. The giant oak tree was unrecognizable as each branch was now a holder for the softness of the falling snow, the thickness of the trunk an arbitrary mixture of whiteness and bark. The sky was an unfolding story of grayness with a predictability of more impending nasty weather.

Talia couldn't remember when she'd seen it snow so much. In some ways it was cozy and she enjoyed the time from work that she wouldn't have typically had. She tried to read, but it was impossible to concentrate while listening to her nephew's excitement at having almost finished building the spaceship she had dreaded doing.

The man sitting on her living room floor should have looked out of place, but he didn't. Every now and then he would look up at her, and she would blush because it was pretty apparent that she had been staring at him, but he would just smile at her, the corners of his eyes crinkling, making the lines there more visible.

Max made her yearn for things she'd never really worried about before.

Soft sheets, strawberries, naked skin, and loving endearments all caressed her mind. However, she guessed that he only saw her as the woman who had saved his ass by giving him somewhere to stay.

Talia laughed to herself. She was glad he couldn't read her mind or he'd be off out the door and into the snow as if the devil himself was after him.

"Look, Aunty Tally."

At the sound of Charlie's voice she came out of her euphoric thoughts and looked into his cute, sparkling eyes. She smiled before looking down at the completed toy.

"Oh wow, Charlie. It looks super-duper."

"Isn't it? Can I go and play with it?"

Of course you can, she assured him. To exit the room, he turned around. "What do you say to Max for helping you"? she inquired, stopping him in his tracks.

"Thanks, Max."These are the best blocks ever.

Then, like Flash himself, he vanished.

Max stood up and went to put a log on the fire. It hissed back at him as he put the guard in front of the flames. He turned around and stood facing her, enjoying the warmth behind him.

"You're very good with him," Talia said

"He's very easy to be with."

Max sat down in the chair opposite where she was and she tried to ignore the constant sexual impact his presence was having on her. It was a feeling she didn't know how to deal with, so she set her book to one side, standing up. "I'll go finish the dishes and make some tea."

She didn't give him time to answer, but she did get a quick glance at the surprised look on his face. Leaving the room, she shut the door behind her and leaned against it for a moment, thankful for the cooler air, before she scurried into the kitchen.

She was washing the last dishes when she heard Max come in, shutting the door. She turned around, her wet hands dripping water everywhere, and Max came over and reached for the dish towel, handing it to her. He was so tall that the kitchen seemed minute with him in it, which made her breathe faster than she should have to.

"Thank you," she said as she dried her hands, then set the towel to the side. "Tea?" she asked him as she switched on the kettle.

Without her even asking he started to dry the crockery from the drainer. The shock must have shown on her face because he looked at her and asked, "What's wrong?"

She smiled. "Nothing, it's just not something that's ever happened in my kitchen."

"What, a man helping?"

She nodded.

"You've known all the wrong men," he said as he continued to dry the dishes.

She watched as those mouth-watering muscles moved beneath the sweater she had borrowed from Mrs. Sweet. The grace in his movements was mesmeric in someone as big as him. And something deep within her tightened in a very annoying lust she seemed to have developed for him. He didn't know that she'd never had a man in her kitchen before.

"But you don't have to do that," she said as she took the dried cups from him and popped a teabag in each.

"I don't mind. It's something I've always had to do."

"Your mum has trained you well," she said.

"My mom died when she gave birth to me, and I spent the latter part of my childhood growing up in a children's home." His expression changed for a single second before it reverted to a smile.

"Oh, I'm so sorry."

He lifted his broad shoulders. "No need, it happened a long time ago."

His navy-blue orbs were mesmerizing, and she had to remind herself not to stare. How could a man look so utterly sexy with his hair disheveled, his jaw dark with his beard? It bothered her somewhat that he made her feel like a woman; not just any woman but a sexy, attractive woman…and she knew she'd never been one of those.

* * * *

Max didn't mind talking about his past, but he figured it wasn't something you did with someone you'd just met. It was strange, but he felt very comfortable with

Talia. Anyway, he didn't want to scare her off. He really liked her. It was ridiculous, because they didn't know each other at all. But he'd known that she was different the first time he'd bumped into her in the hotel lobby.

As he finished drying the silverware, his eye caught something moving outside. He turned his head to look but he couldn't see anything. He frowned for a moment, looking around. It must have been a bird. Talia had her back to him, making the tea, so he stepped toward the window. It must have been a damn big bird, because unless he was very much mistaken there were footprints in the snow.

"Looks like the snow is easing up," Talia said as she handed him a cup of tea.

She was right, it was.

"The phone lines should be back up soon, and you'll be able to get back to the hotel."

He wondered why he found that disappointing. He leaned against the counter and put his cup down, folding his arms across his chest. "I'm sure you'll be glad to get rid of me."

"Not at all. It's been nice having some adult company. Charlie has loved having you here, and if I'm honest, I wasn't looking forward to putting that Lego set together." She smiled and it lit up the room.

All his life he'd wanted nothing more than to be loved. His dad had done his best, but love wasn't one of his many attributes. It wasn't that he didn't care about Max, but his head was always full of inventions and not real life.

Maisy, his friend Jarrod's wife, had given the first idea that love was more than a word. She was a very special woman who loved taking care of everyone. But at the age of thirty-two, he'd never been in love, although he'd come close.

For the first time in his life, he felt vulnerable, and it was because he didn't quite understand why Talia had this effect on him. Max yearned to kiss her on the mouth and remove the awful glasses she was sporting so he could properly see her eyes. If he had done that, he wondered what she would have done. Grimacing, Max was aware that if he tried to act out his fantasy, he would probably get slapped in the face.

"How long have you been working at The Grosvenor?" he asked, realizing she knew more about him than he did about her.

"Not long," she said. "Since coming home I've worked in a few hotels."

"You've been away?"

She nodded but didn't elaborate.

"Charlie is visiting?" he asked, pretty sure that wasn't the case.

"No, he lives with me. I'm his legal guardian. My sister was in a car accident that killed my parents."

"I'm so sorry," Max said sincerely.

She said, "It's sad," and he could see the sorrow on her face. "Tilly, my twin sister, now uses a wheelchair and has brain damage."

"It is sad," she said, and he could see the pain on her face. "Tilly, my twin sister, survived but has brain damage and is confined to a wheelchair."

Talia drew out a chair and sat down. He suddenly noticed how worn out she was. Her skin was pale, and she had dark smudges beneath her eyes that seemed to appear from nowhere. A frown centered at her brow as she sat back, her hands folded in front of her.

She had suffered a terrible loss, and he didn't know what to say in a way that would convey how sad he was for her.

"Do you look after your sister as well?"

"No, she's in a care home not far from here. Charlie doesn't like to go, but we've moved around a few times over the last year, so it's not been easy to take him. It's a lot easier now that we're closer."

"And his dad?"

Fear was not what he was expecting to see in her expression, but there it was.

"My sister wasn't always the best at judging people's morals, and she made a mistake when she met Roy."

He was more interested in how he was going to get more money from Tilly for his drugs than the fact she was pregnant."

"That must have been hard for you."

"Not so much me, but my parents. Unfortunately, Tilly should never have been a mum." She frowned. "I worked away a lot, ninety-nine percent of the time."

"What kind of work took you away so much?"

"I'm an archaeologist." She chuckled at what must have been the look of shock on his face. "I get that reaction all the time," she grinned. "It never gets old."

"So, you were on a dig when the accident happened?"

She nodded. "I was in Greece. Crete to be precise. Pottery is my expertise, Bronze age, early Helladic."

"Do you miss it?"

"I do, but it's not something you do with a nearly six-year-old."

He nodded, understanding how difficult that would be.

"I have a doctorate, and I could lecture in universities, but at the moment it's a little difficult with moving around so much." She stood and pushed her chair under the table. "I'll look into it once Charlie and I are settled."

"You are full of surprises, Dr. Wolf."

For a moment, she looked frightened, sad, and resolute. Talia worried her bottom lip between her teeth. He didn't like the thought that she would be afraid of anything or anybody. She looked away, avoiding his gaze, and when she turned back to him all the emotions he'd seen were gone and she had a smile on her face.

Max had decided that he would see her again, and for some reason he couldn't quite put his finger on, he felt guilty.

His gut instinct told him something was amiss, and he didn't like the fear he'd seen in her face.

* * * *

Talia pushed her trolley around the hotel lobby. It had been a long day. She'd started at 7 AM, and she worked almost as if she was a robot. She hated that she was unable to pursue her life's passion. After attending summer camp, she became addicted to archaeology.

Some of her friends had changed their minds several times about what they wanted to study, but not her. April had gone from wanting to be a famous rock star to a teacher. Talia smiled. April had an influential voice and could easily pull off as a rock star.

April had taken Talia under her wing when they'd met in primary school. She had been the kid with the glasses and uncontrollable hair—which was why she kept it short now—while her sister had always been the beauty and the one who drew friends to her.

Talia hadn't seen Max since he was holed up at her place. He might possibly have gone home by now. She couldn't shed the disappointment she felt at that thought. He hadn't been in touch, and actually, why would he have been?

She'd promised Charlie she'd pick him up from school today and they would go for the Christmas tree they hadn't been able to get on her last day off. Christmas was over a week away and Charlie was so hyped up already. He'd written his final list weeks ago, and fortunately, she'd been able to get almost everything he'd asked for.

Looking at her watch as she shut the door to her last room of the day, she sighed with relief. She had plenty of time to pick her nephew up. She wanted to visit Tilly after they chose their tree and took it home, although she wasn't looking forward to getting it on a bus. She would have to try to persuade Charlie to get a small one. Hopefully, Mrs. Sweet would look after him while she spent an hour with her sister.

These last few days she'd left Charlie with Mrs. Sweet early in the morning when it was dark and came home in the evening when it was dark. It had been snowy and cold, which was to be expected at this time of year, but it normally wasn't as bad as it had been.

This would be the first Christmas that Charlie and she would be on their own. They would visit with Tilly on Christmas Eve. There was no other family, and although she hadn't always made it home for the season, she would feel it more this year.

What was the saying, you don't realize what you

have until it's gone? Talia thought she hadn't had a connection with her parents and sister. It hurt that she hadn't made more of an effort and now it was too late.

Standing at the bus stop to go pick Charlie up from school, she stamped her feet to try and elicit some warmth into them. Glad that she had her hat and scarf on, she shoved her hands into her coat pocket. The bus was late…again!

Across the road, there was a silhouette standing by the hotel tradesman entrance. With the combination of the dark, heavy clouds and the shadow of the streetlight she couldn't see if it was a man or woman. A seriously scared shiver seeped through to her bones, and suddenly Talia had this feeling that it was Roy. But how could he have found them? She had been so very careful.

Talia hitched her bag over her shoulder to stop it from falling down her arm. A car stopped and the passenger side window opened. Thinking it was someone looking for directions, she ducked down only to see Max was in the driver's seat, and he smiled that enigmatic smile he had. But his eyes were weary, and Talia thought he looked tired.

"Hello, Talia."

"Hi, Max. How are you?"

"I'm good, thanks. Are you waiting for a bus?"

"Yes, that's if it ever comes," she said with a slight sense of humor, because she was getting a little panicked as Charlie would be out of school soon. She didn't want to get a taxi because she would need to get one when they went to see Tilly later, and she certainly couldn't afford two taxi fares.

"Hop in, I'll take you home," he said.

"No really, it's fine. I'm going to pick Charlie up

from school."

"If you show me the way, I can do that too."

Talia stood for a second and looked in the direction in which the bus should be coming from. Even after silently pleading for the vehicle to appear, it didn't.

"Are you sure you don't mind?"

"It's the least I can do after what you did for me."

"Okay, thanks," she said as she opened the door to get in. Slipping the seatbelt over her shoulder, she clicked it into place and set her purse on the floor by her feet.

"Is everything all right?" he asked.

She turned her head to look at him. "Yes, I just don't think I can feel my feet."

He narrowed his eyes for a moment as if he could see the fear she'd had only seconds ago, but then nodded and set the car in motion. "Let's do something about that." He turned the car heater on full blast, and within seconds she began to thaw out.

Talia didn't think she could cope with moving again, and certainly, it wasn't good for Charlie to not have a secure home. Why did she keep doing it? She had legal custody of him. There was nothing Roy could do about it. But she was scared of him, and she didn't mind admitting that.

Chapter 5

Max watched as Talia walked toward the school. She had her head down against the biting wind and her hands were dug deep into her pockets. There was something that didn't settle well with him. She was meticulous at trying to hide whatever was bothering her, but he could pick up a strong sense of fear that emanated from her body language.

He kept the car engine running; it was too cold outside not to. Although the snow had cleared there had been a few flurries, but it was the extreme cold that seemed to have the UK turning up their heating. There were lots of people walking toward the school, breath swirling out in front of them.

Max had been so busy the last few days that he'd hardly had time to think about anything but work. That wasn't to say that Talia hadn't been on his mind, because she had. Never before had anyone or anything interrupted his work. When he was working on his designs it seemed as though he was in another world. He didn't need silence or to be cooped up in an office on his own, he just seemed to zone out. His dad had been the same way, and Max had stood in a room many a time and watched how he worked.

Max rubbed the back of his neck. He was completely sure that his dad had never let a woman enter his thoughts. Although from how his dad reacted when he talked about his mom, they'd been in love and it had broken his heart when she had died, so perhaps he had. But for Max it was a new experience. Every time he closed his eyes, he wanted to feel Talia's lips on his. The anticipation was almost too much to bear.

His aim when he came there to re-address his project was to single out the fault and draw up new designs which would accomplish his vision of the new wings that would allow the airplanes to move quicker and stealthier in the field of combat. He had hoped to have finished those by the new year.

He had worked twenty-four-seven, and hopefully, he had achieved that with the new adjustments that were currently being made. He should be packing to go home, and he had every intention of going to see Talia before he traveled back to the states. It would have been nice to take her out for dinner. A long-distance relationship? But no distance would stop him from wanting to see her again.

His mind was brought back to the present by the sight of her and Charlie coming toward him. Turning off the ignition, he got out of the car to greet the running child.

"Hey, Charlie. How are you?"

"Max, it's you."

"Yes, it was when I last looked." He went down on his haunches and was momentarily shocked when Charlie went straight into his arms. But it didn't take him but a second to return the hug.

"Are you coming with us to get a Christmas tree? Aunty Tally said we could go after school."

He wondered how they were going to get a tree home when she didn't seem to have a car. "If it's okay with Talia, I'd love to come." He stood up. "Come on, get in the car," he said as he opened the door.

"You haven't got a booster cushion for me, and I'm too small not to have one." The little boy looked up at him.

"I'll tell you what, I'm sure if we strap you in, you'll be okay for just this once."

Charlie seemed to be processing this before he jumped into the back seat and let Max slip the belt across him and fasten it.

"Okay?" Max asked

"Superb," Charlie replied, and Max almost laughed out loud.

Expecting to see Talia behind him, he shut the door then opened his own to get inside, but as he looked over the roof of the car, he saw her having an intense discussion with a man. In fact, she was trying to shake his arm off. Immediately, Max's protective instincts besieged him, and he shut his door and quickly made his way over to them.

"Is everything all right, Talia?" he asked, standing at her side, well aware that he towered over the man opposite her.

She looked up at him, and relief was predominate in her eyes. "Yes, everything is fine," she said. "Roy was just leaving, weren't you?" Talia said as she returned her gaze to the other man. Her words were spoken in a way that would have given him no option. But he didn't move. His fingers gripped hard as she tried to shake them off, and he laughed in her face.

"I think the lady would like her arm back," Max remarked with not a vestige of humor showing in his expression as he recognized the man's name from when

Talia told him about Tilly's ex-husband.

"What's it got to do with you?" Roy spat back at Max as he rubbed his arm over the thin jacket he was wearing. Max wondered if it was needing his next fix that made him do that and not the cold.

"Well, as you quite clearly pointed out, nothing. However, your son is over there in my car, watching everything you do." Max stepped forward, quietly threatening, "And Talia is my friend, so I suggest you do as she asks."

Roy stared at Talia and opened his mouth in a flurry of words that were clearly threatening, and by the stiff stance of the woman who was next to him he knew that she was afraid of every word that was being spoken.

"If you think for one minute you're going to get away with taking my son, you are deluded."

Keeping her voice controlled, she replied through gritted teeth, "And if you think you're getting your hands on Charlie, you've evidently lost your mind. I'm his legal guardian, and even if I wasn't, do you think any court in this land would let you look after a five-year-old child? For God's sake, Roy, look at you—you can't stand still, your eyes are glazed, and look at your hands."

Max looked down and could see scabs over the skin where the man had tried to put a needle in. Roy shoved his hands into his jacket pockets.

"He's my son," the man opposite Talia said, his words slurred.

Talia, who had been standing well away from Roy, leaned in a little closer. "When was your last drink? How long ago did you inject something into your arm?" she hissed at him. "Sometime today by the way you're trying to hold yourself up," she said as Roy leaned forward, almost as if he was going to fall over.

Max wasn't sure if she would appreciate his interference, but keeping a close eye on Charlie, who was still in the car, he could see the worried look on the child's face.

"I don't really think this is where you should be conducting this kind of conversation," Max said to him.

"What the fuck is it to do with you?"

"Nothing except that there is a little boy over there who is watching this little play you're putting on here."

"I've had enough of this. Roy, I will not be chased off by you anymore. Just leave us alone." Talia hurried over to his car, but before she turned and left the disgruntled man, she had looked genuinely scared of Roy and that made Max's blood boil as he felt a protective streak suddenly appear from nowhere.

"I suggest you do as she says," Max told Roy. And with those words, he walked away and headed to his car.

* * * *

Talia made sure Charlie was okay in the back seat, and by the time Max returned she was already in the car, putting on her seatbelt.

"Who was that man, Aunty Tally?"

"No one, my lovely. I used to know him a long time ago," she said in way of an explanation.

"I don't like him. He was shouting at you," Charlie said in a tone of voice she recognized…without even looking she knew his lip would be pushed out.

Swiveling around so she could see him, Talia put her hand on his leg. "It's fine, Charlie. You don't have to worry about him." She smiled, and although tentative, he smiled back.

"Can we still go get a tree?" he asked, and just like

that, it was forgotten…a child's simple view on life.

She turned back in her seat to look at Max. She knew he must be wondering what was going on. He deserved some sort of explanation, but not now; not in front of Charlie.

"I'm sorry you had to be involved in that. Would you mind taking us home?"

"But Aunty Tally…our Christmas tree," a voice piped up in the back.

Talia could tell from Charlie's tone that he was on the verge of tears, and her heart broke for him. He didn't even know that Roy was his father. She had debated with herself on several occasions if she should tell him or not.

Turning her head so she could see him, Talia smiled at him. "We'll go get one later on the bus." She hoped she'd be a little more steady by then. The incident with Roy had shaken her up, and if she was honest, it had frightened her. She'd been so grateful when Max had come to stand beside her.

"I'll take you to get one," Max said.

"Yes, yes, yes. Please, can we go with Max?" Charlie pleaded as he jumped up and down in his seat.

"You really don't have to." She was thankful that he hadn't said anything about the altercation that had just occurred.

"No, I don't, but I want to, and then perhaps later you can explain to me why that man was shouting at you?" He had lowered his voice toward the end of his words, and she looked at him, about to argue, but she could see in his face that he wasn't going to take no for an answer.

But she didn't owe him anything…yes, she did, and to be honest, it would be nice to share it with someone.

April was great, but Talia didn't want to keep bothering her as she neared the end of her pregnancy, because she had enough going on.

Talia had wanted to visit Tilly tonight, but she would take Charlie to see her tomorrow night, and they would have more time.

She stared back at Max as he waited for her answer. He had started the car, and she could feel the full force of the heater on her body as it finally thawed out.

"Thank you. It certainly would be easier than the bus." Talia had not been looking forward to doing that.

"Perhaps we could get something to eat as well. Are you hungry, Charlie?" Max asked her nephew.

"Hungry, am starving…Maccy Dees, Maccy Dees," he said.

She chuckled at the look of confusion on Max's face. "MacDonald's," she explained.

He laughed. "Sure, Charlie, Maccy Dees it is."

They went for food and then to the garden center to look at trees. It was freezing cold but Charlie didn't seem to notice it as he ran around the trees, looking for one he liked.

The scent of pine was prevalent, and she breathed it in. There were Christmas decorations everywhere. It was a happy place to be. Families were walking around trying to decide on their trees, children were very hyperactive, and everyone loved the music at this time of year. It was like a giant playhouse for children.

"Thank you for this. It has been a fun evening."

"My pleasure. I've enjoyed myself," Max said as they followed Charlie.

She laughed. "You don't have to say that. I feel it's not something you've done before with an almost six-year-old hyperactive child."

"No," he said as he stopped, and she turned to look up at him, her eyes staring at his mouth as he spoke.

Her heart rate quickly tripled, forcing her to take a breath. She felt cold, but suddenly, she was hot. Talia observed the darkening of his pupils when she turned her head back to face him, making it impossible for her to prevent the impending kiss.

He leaned in, and anticipation clutched her as his breath mingled with hers. The closer he got, the quicker her breathing became. It was like slow motion, a whisper, a touch away from feeling those wide, smooth lips on hers.

"Talia," he whispered hoarsely.

"Yes," she replied, her voice sounding as distant as the moon and stars above them in the darkness of the early evening.

"Yuck, are you two going to kiss?" a little boy's voice said.

Talia jumped and almost fell over. If it hadn't been for Max reaching out for her arm, she would have been sitting on the cold ground.

Max got himself together before she did. "Have you found a tree?" he asked Charlie, which was a good call on his part because her nephew had forgotten all about what he'd asked. He put his tiny, warm hand in hers and she wrapped her fingers around it.

"Come on, Aunty Tally. Come and see it."

She followed behind him, having no choice as Charlie held onto her hand so tightly. She could hear Max behind her and refrained from turning around to look at him.

They stopped suddenly, and Charlie stood next to a

tree; not just any tree, but a humungous one.

"Honey, this is far too big for our house." *Not to mention the price*, she thought as she saw the tag.

His face went from smiling to sad in a split second, and she wanted so much to take away that sadness. He'd had more than his fair share of it.

Max must have seen the disappointment on his face. He went on his haunches and looked at Charlie. "This would never get through the front door, buddy. What about the one behind it?"

She looked at the one Max pointed out. It was a little smaller, but *little* was the operative word. Talia couldn't see its price tag, but she was confident she couldn't afford it.

Charlie went to have a look and gave it his approval by jumping up and down. "Yes, yes, this one, it's bushier. Look, Aunty Tally, it already has snow on it," he said as his whole body shook with excitement.

Max stood up. "My treat," he said, "for letting me stay."

"Absolutely not," she said.

"Absolutely yes. Let me do this?"

She frowned. "You don't have to."

"I know, but I want to."

For a moment, she watched as Charlie stood by Max. The little boy placed his hand in Max's, and she looked back up to the surprised expression on his face before he engulfed the small hand in his.

Emotion stung at her eyes. Charlie had bonded with Max, and she was worried about what would happen when he returned to his home in America. Was it cruel? Should she pull him away? But Charlie looked so happy and had so much sadness in his short life.

And instead of saying no, she said, "Okay, thank you."

Charlie was beside himself with excitement, making her laugh.

"You've made a little boy very happy. I hope you'll still smile when you try to get that tree into the front room." She chuckled.

"Umm…perhaps we may have to bend the top a little," he said.

"You think?" she asked, smiling.

"Maybe a lot," he said as he stroked his short beard. He looked down at Charlie who was beaming back up at him. "But it will be worth it."

She saw the excitement emanating from her nephew's body and the pleasure on his face…it was the most memorable moment, and she'd had a few with her work when discovering ancient findings. However, seeing Charlie look like that was priceless.

* * * *

Max had no idea how he had ended up in this circumstance.

He should have hated it, but he was having the time of his life. Maybe he was doing it for himself to experience the joy of Christmas. He knew nothing about families, so what was he doing there?

They'd managed to get the tree into Max's rental Audi Quattro by lifting it off the back shelf in the trunk. Charlie, squished in the back seat beside the top end of the tree, thought it was hilarious that one of the branches kept poking Max in the arm and a pine cone kept jabbing Talia on the back of the head. The scent of pine was a little overpowering in such proximity, but Max loved every minute of the journey back to Talia's. It was fun.

In fact, he was really surprised at how much he enjoyed himself.

Charlie had changed out of his school uniform and into his outside clothes while Talia had gone to the shed to get a saw for Max. There was a smug look on her face as she watched him saw off the top of the tree.

Charlie was cute personified with his red hat half on his head and his wellies on the wrong feet. He complained that he couldn't breathe when Talia wrapped his scarf around his neck, making some huffing and puffing noises. Max felt something shift inside him as Charlie stood there watching him with eyes that twinkled as bright as stars.

Max cleared his throat as he caught Talia looking at him funny.

"Are you okay?" she asked as she bent down to help Charlie put his wellies on the right feet.

"Yeah, sure," he said. "Come on, buddy, let's get this tree inside. You go ahead and show me where it goes."

Lucky for him these Edwardian houses had tall ceilings, so once they got it into the living room it fit fine.

"It still looks too big to me," Talia said with amusement as she picked up the scarf Charlie had thrown on the floor.

Max glanced in her direction and was mesmerized by how she looked. Her usually pale cheeks were flushed from the cold, and her eyes twinkled. If he kissed her now, would her lips be cold?

He met her gaze and she stopped laughing, gazing back at him, and he knew she was thinking the same thing he was—if they kissed now, it would be enough to melt the icy frost settling into the night.

He saw her swallow, and she turned away to drag the box she'd brought from next door over to the tree. "Mrs. Sweet gave me these. As this is our first Christmas together we didn't have any decorations."

"Come on. We need to get these lights out, and they're all twisted," Charlie said as he opened the box, pulling out the tangled mess.

Max looked down at the boy. His blond hair was tousled, and those eyes almost identical to Talia's bubbled with excitement. His enthusiasm was infectious, and Max kneeled to help him unravel the colored bulbs.

As they worked, Charlie chatted about what he'd done in school that day. Talia had set light to the wood on the fire's grate, and now the logs were blazing, spitting out the glowing embers. He had a funny feeling that this was how Christmas was and he felt as though he was looking in through a snow globe. It was a surreal feeling, almost of detachment!

Shaking his head as if to shift the cloud that wouldn't move, he lifted the lights around the tree. "Where do you want these to go, Charlie?"

"All the way around, lots and lots of times," he said as he looked up from the box where he was pulling out decorations to hang. Although, to Max, it appeared as though he was tipping them all out onto the floor, choosing the ones he liked.

"Here, let me help you," Talia said to Max. "It looks like the munchkin here has lost interest in helping you with these." She picked up the end of the lights, giving them to him. Their fingers touched and he thought that his hair must be standing on end as he felt a sizzle of electricity pass through him.

"Hey, you two, why are you staring at each other?

Aunty Tally always tells me it's rude to stare."

For a split second, they both looked at him before laughing.

"Who's the child, him or us?" he whispered to Talia.

She wrinkled her nose. "I'm beginning to wonder."

"Okay, big man, come and help me with these lights."

"I'll go make some chocolate," Talia said, a faint flush staining her cheeks.

"Can I have marshmallows?" Charlie piped up.

"Sure you can."

"Can I?" Max wriggled his eyebrows comically.

"Only if you're a good boy and get those lights up," she replied, amusement twinkling in her eyes.

"Honey, I'm always a good boy," he said, winking.

The flush on her cheeks got redder, and she cleared her throat. "Right, I'll go make hot chocolate," Talia said as she left hurriedly, and he chuckled.

"What's funny, Max?"

"Nothing, bud. Let's get this tree done."

"Yes, yes." Charlie jumped up and down with excitement.

The more time Max spent with these two, the more it made him think about what it would be like to have a family like this. It made his heart heavy for what he didn't have. It wasn't until now that he realized how much he wanted it.

Max had no idea what sort of baggage Talia was transporting, and the man at the school had made it clear that something was amiss. However that didn't stop him from wanting to learn more about what was bothering this woman he felt such a connection with.

He wanted to help.

* * * *

Talia settled a very excited Charlie into bed and read him two stories before he finally gave up the fight. Alfie was tucked into his side as he fell asleep. She'd never seen him so happy. Max was good with him, and Charlie sensed that.

Talia took each stair down slowly as her stomach muscles fluttered a little...a lot. She was more than a little attracted to the man in her living room. She searched her mind for how to deal with it because this was so different from anything Talia had felt.

Taking a deep breath, she pushed the door open. Max was sitting on the sofa, and the flames from the fire cast an orange hue over the room. He'd turned off the main light and switched on the lamps. It looked romantic, but it was far from her mind as she knew he would want answers.

He stood up as she entered, and she wished he'd stayed sitting. He seemed much more prominent, his broad shoulders blocking out the fire.

"Please sit down," she said, slightly embarrassed.

Then, she noticed the two wine glasses and a bottle of wine.

"I hope you don't mind," he said as he sat down. "I was going to make coffee, but then I saw the wine, and I thought you could probably use some."

Talia nodded as she sat on the chair opposite the sofa. "It has been a long and eventful day. I need this," she said as she accepted the glass he'd poured. "Thank you." She sipped the deep ruby liquid and enjoyed the peppery, fruity taste that slipped down her throat.

"Are you okay?" he asked.

Straight to the point. Talia produced a smile. "I'm

fine."

"Really?" His eyes narrowed, and he gave her a knowing look. "Tell me about the guy with the nasty vibes and was displaying an animosity that was not very nice for you or anyone around you."

Max sat back on the sofa and looked perfectly comfortable. She'd never thought about a man, or men; Talia Preferred the company of her work. But when she was with him he made her feel things that hadn't even crossed her mind.

She'd had sex, and it was okay, but not something that left a lasting memory. It had been the other way, which was why she'd decided long ago that her work came first. She understood it; men, not so much.

But all that had changed now. She had Charlie, and he was her number one priority. Talia had to protect him from his raving, lunatic father. Roy didn't seem to understand that she was his son's legal guardian.

Talia could feel Max's gaze on her face, although she couldn't meet his eyes because she felt embarrassed that he'd seen how Roy had intimidated her. Usually, that was not the case, but when Max came over, she'd wanted to get rid of her ex-brother-in-law as quickly and quietly as possible without causing a commotion.

Thankfully, she'd seen Max put Charlie in the car and glanced to see if he had noticed what was holding her back, but he looked busy waving at his friend on the other side of the parking lot.

"Talia," Max said softly. His eyes were kind and caring.

She'd known him for almost no time, yet she felt it had been a lifetime. She couldn't explain what he'd forged inside her mind, and to tell him seemed to be the most natural thing in the world.

She set the glass on the coffee table in front of her and sat on the edge of her seat, hands clenched on her lap, while she found the right way in her mind to start her story.

Her body was tense, but she was careful to neutralize her expression; it was the only way she could find the stamina to go over the entire story.

Max had set his glass down too, but he remained leaned back, his leg crossed over the other as he waited for her to start.

"I told you about the car accident?"

He nodded.

She wanted to reiterate what had happened in more detail. "January of this year, my parents and twin sister were in a car accident. Mum and Dad died, and Tilly was seriously injured."

"It must have been an awful time for you. I'm so sorry, Talia," he said with genuine sympathy. His eyes reflected the warmth from the fire, and although he seemed a little tense, there was nothing to suggest he didn't want to hear her story.

"Charlie is Tilly's son, and the man shouting at me is her ex-husband."

"Charlie's dad?"

"Yes."

"But I'm guessing there's some kind of disagreement going on?"

She nodded. "Apparently—and I say that because I'd had no idea—Tilly had left instructions in her will that if anything happened to her or she was left incapable of making her own decisions I was named Charlie's legal guardian." Talia remembered how shocked she'd been.

"Tilly and I were never really that close, and I'd only seen Charlie when I came home, which wasn't very often. We weren't a close family."

Talia had been staring at her hands rather than him, but when she glanced up he was looking at her.

"Where is your sister now?" Max asked.

"Tilly is in a nursing home not far from here. She needs twenty-four-hour care. In the accident, the car that hit Dad's came head-on, Tilly was in the back seat. She broke her neck and had stopped breathing. By the time paramedics got to her she had been without oxygen, and when they resuscitated her she was left a paraplegic with brain damage."

Talia felt tears prick the back of her eyes. She wasn't close to her sister, but it was a dreadful way to live out your life.

She breathed in deep. "Roy thinks his son should be with him, despite the fact that he's a heroin addict and doesn't seem to have a fixed address." She swallowed. "Charlie has an inheritance that will become his when he turns eighteen." She fought a little to keep her voice steady. The thought of Roy getting anywhere near Charlie made her want to throw up. "Roy thinks he will have access to the money if he has Charlie. He keeps threatening to do me harm. We've moved from place to place for the last eleven months, but everywhere I go he seems to find me."

"And when he does, he threatens you like he was doing earlier. Have you reported him to the police?"

"Yes, I have a restraining order on him, but every time I report him to the authorities, he disappears." Talia breathed in deeply. She was frightened of him; Roy was a horrible man, and when he was high, he was even worse Roy claims that if I give him money, he'll leave us alone. I would if I could, but Tilly's care has already consumed my savings." Her jaw clenched; I've had enough of it. It's not fair to Charlie to keep moving around all the time."

"Even if you had all the money in the world, he would only keep coming back for more."

Her heart sank because she knew he was right.

"So, you're going to stay here?"

Without hesitation, she nodded.

Her learning curve over the past year had been extremely steep. In her little world, Talia had become lost.

But if nothing else, it had made her stronger. Having Charlie had been one of the best things that had ever happened to her. She would never have thought she was the kind of woman who could do what she had to keep going. But she had and would do anything to protect the little boy in her care.

Chapter 6

Max had listened to Talia's story as she recounted the last year, and it had tugged at his heart. It seemed that Talia had taken one blow after another. When she explained about Roy, he'd had a bad feeling that things would get worse before they got better, which was another reason his idea was good.

However, Max didn't get a chance to voice his idea when they both jumped at the sound of knocking on her front door. He looked at his watch. It was almost ten PM.

"Are you expecting someone?" he asked.

"No."

Talia stood up and walked over to the closed living room door, but before she could open it he was behind her, and he put his hand over hers.

"Don't go on your own."

She nodded as the knocking came again, only they heard Mrs. Sweet shouting her name this time. Max quickly opened the door and Talia stepped forward.

"What's wrong?" She took the woman's hand and drew her inside the hallway.

"Oh, Talia, thank goodness you're here. Your shed is on fire. I've phoned the fire brigade, and they're on their way."

"Oh my God." She went running out the door and around to the back of the house before Max could stop her.

"Talia, wait," he called after her. He glanced at Mrs. Sweet. "Can you keep an eye on Charlie?"

"Yes, yes…go after her," she said.

That is precisely what he did.

As he moved toward the fire, he felt the heat of the flames. He couldn't move fast enough as he saw Talia standing, just staring at it. He immediately took her hand, drawing her further back, and she looked up at him in surprise.

"There's nothing you can do now, honey. Let the firemen do their job," he said as they came up the garden with a hosepipe. Both of them observed the flames being put out, leaving behind a stinking, smoldering heap with clouds of black smoke filling the atmosphere.

"Charlie." She made to go back to the house, but Max laid a hand on her shoulder. "It's okay. Mrs. Sweet is there."

She nodded. They had both forgotten to put coats on, and it was freezing. When she shivered, he put his arms around her. Without any hesitation, she let him look after her.

"It's out now," a fireman told them. He questioned them about the shed's contents, but nothing could have sparked such a fire. "Could be some kids," the firefighter said. "Thankfully, it's not attached to anything, so the damage has been minimal, but it looks like you'll need a new shed."

"Thank you," Max said as Talia seemed to be in a trance. "We appreciate you coming out so quickly."

No issues. So that the station is aware that there was a crime in the area, I'll file a police complaint.

We always get this with kids who have nothing better to do."

The firefighter made his way up the garden, and Max took Talia's hand and followed him around. When they entered the house, Mrs. Sweet was in the front room by the fire. Fortunately, Charlie had slept through the entire ordeal.

"Thank you for staying, Mrs. Sweet," Talia said.

"Oh, my goodness, child, are you all right?" she asked, as she hugged Talia.

"Yes, I'm fine."

But Max knew she was far from fine.

"Did they say how it started?"

"They think it may be kids."

"I don't know what's wrong with society. These kids have nothing better to do, and we have children bringing up children…that's the problem," she said as she made her way toward the front door. "I'll leave you in the capable hands of this big, strong-looking man," she said as he opened the door for her.

Max watched from the doorway, ensuring she returned to her own home. She waved at him from her doorstep before disappearing. He turned around to see Talia climbing up the stairs checking on Charlie.

Max stood by the fire as his idea mulled around in his mind. It was crazy. His friends would think he'd lost his mind. He should clear it with Jarrod and Maisy first, but he knew they would be okay with it once he explained what had happened.

Charlie would love Elsa and her pups that were now three months old. Max didn't like the thought of leaving Talia here on her own. He didn't think for one moment that the fire had been an accident. He had a funny feeling Roy was behind it, trying to scare her into giving him money.

Christmas was only a few days away, and Max had called Jarrod last night to say he'd be coming home. Maisy was over the moon.

It would be hard to get airline tickets, but he would see what Talia said first before looking. If she said no, he would stay right where he was.

Max had some contacts here in the UK. He'd met them when they had been doing the security on the project he'd invented. It was his newest brainchild and it had taken five years to design his latest fighter jet .

The two guys had been in The Secret Boat Service, part of the Royal Navy.

When they'd finished their tours, they signed off and started a security firm that did more than the name suggested. He'd give them a call tomorrow. Even if they couldn't do anything until after Christmas, it would at least set things in motion.

Today at the school, Roy was abhorrent; he'd been on something, intoxicated. His speech sounded slurred and he could hardly keep upright. At one point, Max thought the guy was going to fall over.

Talia had given the impression that she was frightened, which was why he'd gone over to see if she was okay. Roy had been very aggressive with her. Max hadn't liked that one bit. He hated it when men thought they could bully a woman and thought they had every right to be that way. As far as he was concerned, it was cowardly, giving men, in general, a bad name.

He went and sat on the sofa; the burning logs gave out a heat that warmed the entire room. The Christmas tree glittered with lights and decorations. Charlie had loved doing it, and Max had as well. It was a little too tall for the room, but what the heck? It had been worth it to see the little boy giggle with that childlike, endearing sound.

Just then, Talia came in, shutting the door behind her. She looked at Max, and he could see the pain in her eyes. She had those spectacles covering her eyes, but he could tell they were sad.

* * * *

Talia went and perched on the end of the easy chair opposite Max. What had happened? Had Roy really gone as far as to set fire to the shed? Talia knew he could do anything, but she hadn't believed he would stoop so low to get what he wanted.

How on earth was she ever going to get away from him? If she made a stand, it was clear that he would stop at nothing to get what he wanted. Roy thought that by having Charlie, he would get the inheritance. She had told him numerous times that he wouldn't be able to touch the money, but he thought everyone was like him—greedy, selfish, scum on the earth. She had no idea what her sister had ever seen in him.

"I appreciate tonight. Charlie enjoyed himself a lot. I'm sorry you became involved in anything unrelated to you.

She smiled. "You can go now. I'm sure you'll be glad to return to the hotel."

"Talia, how can I leave you when you and Charlie's lives are at risk? You should report it to the police."

"What's the point? The fire service is going to do it. I can't prove Roy set fire to the shed."

"Do you think it was kids?" he asked.

She shook her head. "No, I don't."

"Then I'm not going anywhere, but I have a proposition for you."

Talia listened while Max told her what his plan was. It sounded so good; it would be lovely to get away from worrying about what was happening around her, and Charlie would love it.

But she couldn't go.

"I'm sorry, Max…thank you so much for even thinking about us, but we can't go."

"Why not?" he asked with a questioning look.

"This is Charlie's first Christmas without my parents and his mum. I want to be able to take him to see Tilly. That will be hard for both of us, but mostly the little boy lying in bed upstairs." She swallowed. "I can't let Roy dominate my life. If I don't take a stand now, we will be forever running, and I'm not willing to do that anymore." She'd decided that the fire, which she was almost a hundred percent sure Roy had lit, would not scare her into going on the move again.

"And there is nothing I can do to change your mind?"

"No." It was a simple answer to what had become a severe problem. She was composed in her body stature, but inside, she was crying loudly. She was frightened of what would happen next.

The December wind had increased, rattling the cheap window frames, the cold creeping through the walls. Shivering, she got up and put another log on the fire. She'd just paid to have some delivered to her shed. It would have been enough to get her through Christmas. Now she had nothing except what was on the back porch.

She looked at Max as she sat back down on the threadbare chair that sagged and creaked with her weight. He was frowning as if trying to work something out. The only sound was the Christmas lights clicking as they switched to different programs and the crackling of the wood burning on the hot, red ash.

Talia could still smell the burning smoke from the fire, and she couldn't wait to get under the shower to remove the stinky scent. She really wanted someone to hug her hard and tell her everything was going to be okay.

But that was excessive. Talia had no notion of how to improve things or choose wisely. Everything seemed to be working against her. Her skills as a replacement mother were at zero because it had thrown her into a life she didn't know how to live.

"It's going to be all right, Talia," Max whispered in her ear as he sat on the arm of the chair.

She didn't even realize she had tears until he handed her a tissue. She must look awful. When she cried, her nose turned red and her eyes scrunched like a pug dog. She took her glasses off, laying them on her knee as she wiped her tears.

Max was friendly, and she instantly felt better when he put his arm around her. Without thought, she leaned into him, and it seemed like it was the most natural action in the world. It meant nothing, he was just being kind. The loneliness she felt seemed to dissipate by him doing that one reassuring movement.

April had been a great friend. Talia knew she only had to ask for help and April would drop everything to come to her aid. But her friend was expecting her first child. She had her own life with a husband that she loved.

Talia stayed where she was for a moment, allowing herself for a little while to feel reassured. When he removed his arm she felt bereft. He sat on the coffee table and faced her.

She looked at him as he took her hands into his, smoothing his thumbs up and down her wrists. Talia held her breath for a second before trying to breathe normally, which was hard when he touched her in that way.

He kinda rocked her foundation, which was already on unstable ground. Her heartbeat thudded inside her chest, and she was glad he couldn't see its erratic movements.

"I'm sorry this is happening to you, baby."

Baby?

"We haven't known each other long, have we?"

"No," she whispered.

"I want to help."

"You have helped, more than you'll ever know."

"I don't want you or Charlie going anywhere on your own. When does he finish school?"

"He finished last week but went to a school facility for working mums."

"Okay, there will be no need to do that, I'll take care of him when you can't."

She frowned. "I can't let you do that," she said, sitting up straight.

"Why?"

"Because you have your plans."

"I was going to go home, but I can work from here. As I said before, I don't have any family. My mom died when I was born and my dad passed away when I was fourteen. I spent the next four years in a children's home where I met Liam and Jarrod, who are still my best friends. So, you're not keeping me from anyone or anything." He let go of one of her hands and rubbed the back of his neck.

She felt overwhelmed, both by his loss and her

predicament.

"Come here," he said, taking her glasses and laying them on the table before he stood up.

She looked up at him, but her legs refused to move until he drew her up by the hand he was still holding. Max stroked down her spine, his hand gently pressing her closer to him. She tried to resist, but only for a minuscule second before she curved herself into him. When he kissed her temple she felt the firmness of his lips against her skin like a burst of twinkling lights.

The varying reactions left her confused, and she guessed she was vulnerable. What other explanation could there be? She was being genuinely pathetic, and she hated that he was seeing her this way.

"Come on, let me ensure the house is secure while you get me some bedding." He let go of her, but only to take hold of her hand, and she followed him like some meek female.

She stopped at the door and tried to pull her hand away. "I'm fine, really I am. You can go back to the hotel, or America, or whatever you were planning on doing before you got caught up in all my problems."

He raised his fingers beneath her chin until her gaze met his. "If you think I'm leaving you alone to deal with that lunatic, you are seriously delusional."

"I managed fine before you turned up," she said. The blatant lie made her face feel red and overheated.

"You have managed remarkably well on your own, but what is the point in struggling when I'm offering to help out." He narrowed those navy-blue eyes. "I want to do this, and I'm not taking no for an answer."

It felt too good accepting his help, but perhaps if it was just over Christmas…just a few days of help. Did that make her a bad person? Talia didn't need him, she wanted him. She knew that the first day that he nearly knocked her over in the hotel, there was something between them. The sizzle of chemistry was something she'd never felt before.

"Okay," she said. "Thank you."

He smiled, and it touched her heart as if he had kissed it. When he cupped her cheek she almost melted in front of him like a teenager.

"You're not alone, Talia."

* * * *

Talia made her way out of the hotel, having completed her final shift until after the holidays, and the thought of it felt good, because she was exhausted. She hated feeling so pathetic, so out of control with her life.

Roy would seem to show up whenever she relaxed her guard. He wanted what his son could provide for him; he wasn't interested in Charlie.

She guessed he thought he'd have access to his inheritance if he had his son. That was the amount of intelligence he had. There was no way she would ever give up her nephew.

Every time she moved, Roy showed up. She reported it to the police, but even with the restraining order on him, there was nothing they could do until she could prove he was the one doing all these things to her. Setting fire to her shed was a sure sign that he was escalating, and it frightened her. Dread crawled inside her. What was he going to do next?

All day, Max had been with Charlie. He claimed that anything he needed to do would be achieved anywhere using his laptop.

. When Talia's nephew found out he was staying

with Max he whooped and clapped. To say he liked this man who had come into her life like some guardian angel was an understatement. And he wasn't the only one—she did too…she liked him a lot.

Talia opened the door which led onto the side street. It was a little scary. She hated feeling like that but took a breath before stepping outside. The streetlight didn't fully penetrate the darkness. A breeze was rustling the bin bags in the large container.

Talia shivered, and not only from the cold. The back entrance to the hotel was used by employees and for deliveries, and Talia had stepped out of it many times, but after last night she was being very cautious. There was a far-off siren, and raised voices from the kitchen. She swallowed as she quickly looked around before hurrying with her head down.

All Talia wanted was to get the hell out of the horrible darkness with only a streetlamp for light. Focusing on moving out of the alleyway as quickly as possible, Talia nearly had a heart attack when she hit something hard and a powerful pair of hands grabbed her upper arms, stopping her in her tracks.

"Hey, slow down," Max's familiar voice said.

She took a second to calm her breathing before looking up and seeing the concerned expression on his face. She smiled with relief, and just for a comforting second, she let her hands stay on his chest .

"Aunty Tally, I've had a great day," Charlie piped up, standing beside Max.

She pushed away from the big man in front of her and picked up the little boy, hugging him hard.

"Aunty Tally, you're squeezing me too tight," he said.

She leaned back, looking at his face, and she almost laughed out loud at his expression, his lips tight, his beautiful eyes scrunched up.

"Sorry, honey, but I'm so happy to see you."

"I'm happy to see you too, Aunty Tally, but I like breathing."

She loosened her grip on him before setting him down until his feet touched the ground.

"Phew," he said. "I thought you would squeeze all the air out of me."

She did laugh out loud then. She took hold of Charlie's hand as they followed Max to his car, parked on the opposite side of the road. He opened the car's back door so Charlie could get in, and she got the shock of her life when he climbed onto a booster seat.

She strapped him in before shutting the door. Max was standing with her door open, and before getting in she looked up at him. "You bought a seat for Charlie?"

"Yes, we went and shopped for one today. The salesperson assured me it was the best one to buy?"

"It's perfect. Thank you." She frowned. "Why are you being so good to us?"

He inclined his head. "Because I like you…a lot, and Charlie."

Talia didn't know what to say to that except the truth. "I like you too."

"Good. Come on, let's get out of this cold. Get in the car, baby."

And she did. It was lovely to have someone care, something Talia had never been bothered about. She was so independent, her job had made her that way. It always felt good to be self-supporting and on her own, and she'd never had any problem with being alone for long stages.

There was a gust of wind as Max opened the driver's side door and got in. He started up the engine, and the heater immediately blew out warm air. She slipped on her seatbelt after setting her bag on the floor. Max put the car in motion, and she listened with a smile as Charlie told her with some excitement about everything he and Max had done.

Typically when she walked through the door at the end of the day, the house was in darkness. Today when she entered the hallway, there was a smell of cooking.

She walked past the living room and noticed the golden flames in the fireplace

The house was warm and inviting.

Taking off her coat and scarf, she laid them over the stair banister as Charlie ran ahead of her with Max following him. Walking through the kitchen, she stood gaping at what was in front of her. Garlic wafted with the scent of spices with meat sizzling, and she breathed it in appreciatively.

"Look, Aunty Tally, me and Max cooked dinner." He pulled out a chair for her to sit at the laid-out table, and the excitement on his face was infectious.

"Max and I," she said automatically. "How clever you are helping."

"Max did the cooking, and I did the table."

"It looks perfect," she said as she sat down.

Charlie took his coat and wellies off. He was about to leave them where they were when he picked them up and put them away on the back porch.

Holy cow…

Max smiled at her.

"Thank you," she said.

"No need."

"Yes, there is. I always seem to be thanking you," Talia said, realizing how much of an impact this man had made in her life. "Charlie likes you."

"I like him too. I like his aunty even more."

She could feel her face heating up. No one had ever looked at her in such a way. She licked her dry lips as a natural reaction when Max stared at them with desire in his eyes.

Scarlet heat caressed her cheeks and she imagined herself melting, just sliding to the floor in a puddle of lust and hormones raging with desire. And like a bucket of ice water, Charlie returned to the room.

Phew!

"You and Max are having chili con carnie—which is a silly name to give minced beef—and I'm having the same but with no chilies in it, because Max said they would burn my mouth so hot that I would need ice to cool it."

Talia laughed. "You're quite right, it is a silly name, and Max is right, it would be very hot."

"Charlie, do you want to carry the garlic bread to the table?" Max asked as he took it out of the oven. He sliced it and set it in a small dish. Charlie held it tight in his tiny hands as he walked over and put it in the middle of the table.

"Well, this is so nice," she said to them both.

"I told Max that you deserve it because no one ever cooks for you and I'm not big enough to do it."

Talia cupped his cheek. "You're such a sweet boy."

"Max told me that a girl likes to be taken care of, so that's what we're doing tonight. Aunty Tally, we're going to look after you."

Her heart constricted and she barely held back the

tears. Max smiled at her and just like that they seemed to become something more, a feeling of being part of a team and not on her own.

It wasn't that she was a woman who needed a man to take care of her. She'd been independent since the day she'd left home for university. Talia had always taken pride in how she worked. She always knew what to do and how to do it, but with Charlie…jeez, it had been so hard to adjust to being responsible for a child when she was only ever used to looking after herself.

Max laid out their food on the table in bowls accompanied with rice. The smell was delicious. Talia didn't understand why Max was helping them in this way. Charlie already adored him, and she appreciated the ability to talk to an adult while they ate.

"Do you like it, Aunty Tally?" Charlie asked.

The anticipation on his face was so adorable. Talia had scraped the last of the food into her mouth. "It was lovely. Thank you." She looked at Max. "And thank you. I didn't expect you to do this."

"My pleasure." He smiled at her.

"Max says it's nice to make someone feel special by doing something nice," Charlie spoke with hero-worship in his voice for a man they barely knew.

"He's right." She said as her brow furrowed with worry. Oh dear, was Charlie getting too attached to him?

She gave Max a curious glance and saw something that she didn't recognize as he looked at Charlie and then at her. He wore jeans and a sweater almost the same color as his eyes.

"Can we go and see Mummy? I've made her a Christmas present."

Oh! This was the first time he'd asked to go see her

instead of Talia having to persuade him. Before she could reply, he spoke again.

"Max helped me write her a card, and I drew a picture for her. May I be excused so I can get it to show you?"

"Of course you can, honey."

He jumped from his chair, scooting past her as he ran out the door.

"I hope you didn't mind?" Max said to her.

"Not at all. I'm surprised Charlie told you about her."

"We were talking about doing nice things to help out and he just came out with it."

She thought she saw Max's eyes water up.

"When he told me about his mom, he was so sad that I suggested doing something nice for her."

"Oh, Max, if you only knew how many times I've tried to get him to talk about what happened."

"Jeez, Talia, I'm sorry."

"Don't be daft. I'm happy he's finally found someone to talk to...thank you."

He put his hand over hers which was on the table. "Are you sure you're okay with it?"

Talia turned her hand in his and closed it shut. "Yes, I am."

Her breath quickened at the feel of his elongated fingers as they tightened. His eyes became hooded, partially hiding the electric blue that she knew was there, as myriad emotions seemed to cross his face.

They drew apart when Charlie could be heard running along the hallway, and her skin tingled just from that solitary touch. He came into the kitchen like a herd of elephants and shoved into her hand a large piece of paper that had been folded into two. There was a snowman next to a Santa Claus on the front, and inside it said *Happy Christmas, Mummy*. Tears fell down her cheeks.

"Don't you like it, Aunty Tally?"

She took the little boy's face in her hands and smiled. "I love it, Charlie. It's the best card I've ever seen."

"Really?"

"Really," she said. "Why don't I put it somewhere safe until we go tomorrow night?"

He nodded. "It's Christmas Eve, and Mummy will love it, won't she?" There was a little bit of doubt in his voice.

"She will, sweet boy."

"Okay, young man, I think we should clear away these dishes," Max said.

Chapter 7

Max had ushered Talia into the living room. He'd seen how emotional she'd been when Charlie had brought down the card he'd helped him make for his mom. Max hoped he hadn't overstepped his boundaries. It was an innocuous gesture on his part.

Charlie talked non-stop as they cleared away the last of the dishes, and Max chuckled. He was bewildered at how many conversations could come from one little person.

"Why did Aunty Tally look like she was going to cry when I showed her my card for Mummy? Did I make her sad?"

Max looked at the child's face; it was so innocent, but his young eyes were worried. "You made your aunty very happy," he assured the little boy. "They were tears of joy, not sadness."

"I'm confused. How can you tell the difference?"

How could you indeed? It took years of trying to figure a woman out, and just when you thought you had something knocked you for a loop, leaving you totally confused.

"Sometimes you just know, but it takes a lot to understand a woman."

"I know, right? I don't think I ever will," he said with his eyes scrunched up and his lips pursed.

Max laughed out loud. "You and me both, buddy."

Max finished wiping down the counters while Charlie went to sit with Talia. That boy was getting under his skin, like his Aunty Tally was. It was Christmas Eve tomorrow and he was supposed to be at Nags Head with his friends, but he was here. Trying to explain to Maisy had been the worst inquisition he'd ever had. She'd given him strict instructions to bring them both to meet her and Jarrod as soon as he could.

Liam had been sarcastically funny on the phone, or thought he was, but Max had laughed at his innuendo about being the next one to fall, and how that would never happen to him. *Bastard!*

Max made his way into the living room to squeals of laughter. He never thought in a million years that he would ever like that sound. Max stood in the doorway and watched them both play fight on the floor, Charlie sitting on top of Talia as she tickled him.

Molly sat looking at them as if they'd lost their minds. On seeing Max, she came and wrapped herself around his legs, purring, and he leaned down to stroke her as he watched the hilarity.

He hadn't previously seen this side of Talia. A smile of fun, love, and enjoyment replaced the worry that appeared permanently etched on her face.

He paused for a moment to take in the spectacle in front of him before Charlie caught his attention.

"Max, we've been waiting for you to watch a DVD," he said as he climbed off Talia to go get the film in question.

Max offered his hand, and she took it, he pulled her up close to his chest. Automatically, his fingers spread across the base of her spine.

"You do realize that the film is *The Grinch*," she

said breathlessly.

He bent low so he could speak into her ear. "I don't mind sitting with you as long as I can." Max smiled at her.

"Deal," she said, and they stood like that for a second.

"Come on, you two. I've put it into the player and it's about to start."

They stepped away from each other to see Charlie sitting down waiting for them with the remote in his hand and the biggest smile Max had ever seen.

Charlie patted either side of him. "Aunty Tally, you sit on this side, and Max, you sit here."

After they were all sitting on the sofa, squished together, Molly curled up on the floor next to the fire. She barely opened her eyes when the film came on.

"This is fun, isn't it?" Charlie said, giggling, bouncing up and down between them.

Talia smiled at him. "It is, but you need to settle down or we won't hear what's going on."

"Don't be silly," he said, picking up the remote. "If you can't hear it, just turn up the sound."

Max almost laughed out loud—six years old going on twelve. As they settled down, Max felt more comfortable than ever. When was the last time he sat down like this and watched a movie? He couldn't even remember.

The lights were off, and Talia lit some candles that had a nice Christmas scent, reminding him of cinnamon and cranberries. The glow from the fire set the scene, and to an outsider, they looked like a family. When Max was a child, his longing for something like this had been overwhelming at times. He stopped wishing for it until he realized his dad just wasn't like that.

Charlie was quiet beside them, and three-quarters of the way through the movie Max felt him rest his head on his shoulder. Max lifted his arm to put around him and brought Charlie close.

Talia snuggled closer to the little boy, and Max stretched his arm further to stroke her silky hair. It was satisfying to sit there and feel them both close to him, safe and happy. He liked that…very much.

The credits were on the screen and he had been so enamored by his feelings that he had missed the latter part of the film. Max gently removed himself from the two of them, and picking up the remote off the coffee table, he switched the television off. Turning back around, he reached for Charlie, lifting him in his arms, and took him to bed.

"Is the film finished?" Charlie asked, his voice heavy with sleep.

"It is. Where are your pajamas, buddy?"

"Under my pillow," he said as Max set him on the edge of the bed.

Quickly, he changed him into the blue PJs and drew back the covers for him to lay down.

"Night night, bud," Max said, smoothing his hair back from his forehead.

"Night. I had the best time," he said as he turned on his side and put both hands under his cheek. *God damn*, it made his heart feel like it was overflowing with emotion for this little boy. Max saw a teddy beside him and tucked it under the covers.

Max stared at him for a second before leaving the room and going back downstairs. Talia had curled her long legs beneath her and was fast asleep. Taking the

DVD out, he put it into the sleeve and back on the shelf with all the others.

Max put a log on the fire and went to the CD player he'd seen in the corner of the room. He stopped to look at the photos on a shelf above the CDs. The one that caught his eye was Talia and Tilly together. They were so different that he would never have recognized them as twins. Sisters, yes, but not twins.

He looked at her CD collection, and it pleased him to see they had similar tastes. Choosing one, he slipped the disc from its pocket and put it on. Jazz music was like a painting; somehow, after hearing a few notes, you had a picture in your mind playing a story. You could almost imagine yourself a smoky bar in New Orleans or sitting on the beach watching the sun sink into the blue ocean. He'd always appreciated Miles Davis and had many vinyls of his music at home.

Max went over to the window to check outside. He couldn't see anything, but there was a weird sensation that someone was out there, and he couldn't explain what it was. The information Max received about Charlie's father from his friend Fireball was exactly what he had anticipated. He quickly picked up his phone from the coffee table after it ping-taped with a text.

Speak of the devil, it was a message from Fireball saying he had put someone outside the house for the night to keep an eye on things. That made Max feel a lot better in respect of keeping Charlie and Talia safe.

Quickly, he texted his thanks and put his phone back on the table. He sat down next to Talia. Max thought about how much his life had changed quickly and for the better. The sight of the beauty in front of him had his heart racing in his chest, and he focused on slowing it down.

Mad had no idea why he felt that way or the protective shield he wanted to put around Talia and Charlie, but he was beyond the *why* he was ready for the *do*'s, and he wanted to kiss her from head to toe. His heart filled with emotion, and for a moment, he theorized a family scenario and found that it was something he liked the thought of very much.

Talia opened her eyes, and after a few moments, she smiled at him. Sitting up, she stretched her neck, her creamy, soft skin on show. God, all he wanted to do was feel that skin beneath his lips.

* * * *

Talia stretched. It took a few seconds for her to realize the film had finished and the music was playing.

She turned to look at Max. "Where's Charlie?"

"Bed. He fell asleep too."

"I'm so sorry," she said, sitting up straighter. "Was he all right?"

"What are you sorry about?"

"That you had to do that?"

"Take him to bed?"

"Hey, I didn't mind at all, and yes, he was fine," Max said.

They were so close that she could smell the citrusy scent she associated with him. She breathed it in quietly; how embarrassing if he knew what she was doing. It sounded crazy even to her own ears. Talia hadn't really made time for men, and to be honest, romance had never been exceptionally high on her list of priorities.

But that was before she'd met Max. He brought out desires and feelings Talia had never had before. Sex was sex, an itch that she hardly ever needed scratching. After all, that's what vibrators were for, right?

Damn, there she was thinking about sex when she should be thinking about how she would deal with Roy. Just the thought of his name was enough to make her shudder. He gave her the creeps, and had done so since the first day Tilly brought him home.

Max reached his hand over, palm up, with a faint smile on his lips. Talia laced her fingers with his, and he lifted their hands to his mouth, kissing her knuckles. It was impossible to stop her heart from doing a hop, skip, and jump. Every skin cell tingled, and every neuron fired, leaving her breathless.

"Don't be concerned; we'll figure it out. Roy need not approach you or Charlie."

The feel of his lips pressed onto her skin and the caring tone in his voice very nearly undid her. Max was like a lifeline she'd never needed before, but now when she could feel herself falling apart, his presence meant she was keeping the seams just about together.

How could she have gone from being a single, independent archaeologist who loved her work, to a mum with a crappy job that she hated? And to top it off, she was on the run from a raving lunatic who terrified her. Her throat was thick with emotion, but she couldn't let Max stay here at this time of year…it would be selfish of her.

Talia sat up, taking her hand from his. "Why are you helping us?" She pinched the bridge of her nose before looking back up at him. "You should be home with your friends, especially at this time of year. I can't let you ruin your Christmas holidays."

His forehead furrowed; he was probably questioning his own actions, and who could blame him? Talia bit her lip, because quite honestly, she didn't want him to go. He made her feel safe, but the conflicting emotions that ran through her body told her it was more than that.

"Let's get one thing straight—I want to be here. I like you, and I like Charlie."

She'd noticed that his eyes could turn different dark shades of blue, and at the moment they were a beautiful azure blue like the waters at the Pori beach in Ano Koufonissi.

"Come here," he said, taking her hand as he drew her back into his open arms.

Talia hesitated for a second before she leaned back, and his arms surrounded her as she put her head on his chest. It felt like the most natural place in the world to be, and she could hear the steady beat of his heart next to her ear. On the other hand, hers is pounding like a set of drums to a rock song.

Max pressed a warm, firm kiss to her temple as his fingers clasped around her hand and his arm held her close beside him.

Talia felt the kiss on every part of her, and although she knew it was crazy she wanted more, which only confused her.

She'd always been so independent, and it seemed odd to rely on someone else for a feeling of safety and security, but that's how Max made her feel. She should pull away, but she didn't want to. It wouldn't hurt to be in this man's arms for a while. So she let herself relax, leaning comfortably into him. She loved his beard and had an almost irresistible urge to touch it, but she didn't have the nerve. After all, he was comforting her, wasn't he?

"Do you think Roy will come back?" she asked.

"You know him better than me, but I don't think we've seen the last of him."

She shivered at his words.

"Don't worry. I'm here and won't let anything happen to either of you."

Talia pushed away from him so she could look at him. "Thank you. I was trying to be brave when I decided to stay put and run no more, but I didn't know he would do something like this." She swallowed. "I mean, jeez, setting fire to the shed it's too close for comfort."

"It might not have been him," Max said. "But I find that highly unlikely, considering what you've told me about him and what I saw today."

"Do you fancy a glass of wine?" she asked, getting up from the sofa and stepping toward the door.

"Okay, sounds good to me," he said.

Turning the handle, she stepped out of the room and shut the door behind her. She leaned against it for a moment and took a deep breath before heading into the kitchen. Turning on the light, Talia glanced around the room. Yes, she was checking; it didn't hurt to be careful!

Talia was reaching for the glasses that were too high and was about to get a chair when she felt a body behind her. She reacted like someone demented and pushed away, using her elbows. She heard a whoosh of breath, then turned around to see Max holding his belly.

"Oh my God, I'm so sorry," she said as she went over to him.

"I think we can safely say you can defend yourself," he said with a smile.

"It was a silly thing to do. What were you doing anyway, sneaking up behind me like that," Talia said, losing her sympathy for him.

Max stood up straight. There was no discomfort in his expression; she did not doubt that he'd been pretending and she hadn't hurt him.

"I came to see if you needed some help," he said as he reached around her, removing two glasses from the top shelf.

"I would have gotten a chair."

"Now you don't have to."

His mouth slid into a warm smile, and for some reason, she blushed. They were close, so she didn't stop him when he lifted a hand up to toy with her hair.

"You have hair the color of honey on a warm, sunshiny day," he said before unhooking her glasses from her ears. "I've wanted to take these off since the first time I saw you. Your eyes are like a smooth amber stone with flecks of wisdom and innocence." Taking her by surprise, he brushed her lips with his and gently pushed her backward until her body came into contact with the countertop.

Talia heard the slight noise of her glasses being set down behind her before Max cupped her face with his warm, slightly calloused hands, kissing each eye closed. She loved the feel of his breath on her skin. Unable to resist, she lifted her mouth to his until their lips touched again.

Talia enjoyed the soft, gentle searching as they tentatively explored the feel of each other's lips...until his kiss deepened and became more intense, devouring her mouth with sweeping strokes of his tongue, his beard tickling her nose.

He slipped his hands from her face to her shoulders, slowly smoothing them over her skin and down her back until they reached the base of her spine. He pushed her closer to him so that every intricate part of him touched her and she felt every nerve in her body tingle.

Talia didn't have much experience where men were concerned, but when his tongue touched hers she almost stopped breathing at the way he turned that one kiss into the most passionate one she'd ever had.

She lost herself at the moment's pleasure, encompassed inside a gentle strength, the aura of his scent and the desire for more releasing a hunger for the passion she'd never felt before.

Jeez, her internal temperature was overheating by the second. Talia's hands were compressed against his chest. but she didn't mind because she could feel the muscles beneath his shirt. It surprised her to find them trembling, but his heartbeat was steady and robust, unlike hers, beating at a hundred miles per second.

One of his large hands strayed down to her bottom where he squeezed the cheek of her butt while his other gripped her hip. Talia gave a low moan.

Slowly, Max drew away from her lips, but leaned his forehead against hers. "Damn," he breathed out.

He was still stroking her behind, keeping her near as they both caught their breaths, but just having him this close was not helping her heartbeat return to normal. He loosened his hold, and she felt bereft at the loss of his touch.

"I'm sorry, I shouldn't have taken advantage of your emotional state."

She felt more relaxed than she had in a long time. "You didn't."

"Are you okay?"

She nodded. "Oh yes."

Talia didn't tell him that her body was overheating

from so much need, intoxicating, undiluted lust, and her face warmed as hot as the rest of her felt.

"I guess we got carried away," he said as he bent down to kiss her again; soft, warm kisses that enveloped every sense she had of what kissing meant with the right person. "Your lips are just as soft and sweet as I knew they would be," he said. "And your ass fits inside my palms perfectly." As if she needed a demonstration, Max squeezed her flesh again.

Boy, she didn't need reminding of how good it felt. "No man has ever told me that before."

He cocked his head as he looked at her. "You've obviously been seeing the wrong men," he said before hugging her.

She had no idea what to say to that as the sheer maleness of him overwhelmed her.

He smoothed his thumb across her jaw. "Let's take this into the living room." He kissed her once, twice, three times before passing her the bottle from the countertop where she had left it as he took hold of the two glasses and her hand.

Max let go of her, but only to turn off the light for a second. Heat curled in her abdomen as joy bubbled up inside her. She felt like the teenager she'd never had any interest in being.

Returning to the living room, they both took a seat on the couch, As Max poured the wine she listened to the sounds of the crackling fire and the whistling wind, but they were faint compared to how loud her heart was thumping in her chest.

Molly was fast asleep in her usual place, a small hooded basket she loved to hide in. The whole scenario was perfect…but perfect always went wrong, didn't it?

He handed her a glass of wine as he leaned back beside her. "Here's to…" He hesitated, as if trying to find the right words. "Here's to a great Christmas and an exciting New Year." He touched her glass with his, and the tinkling sound of glass on glass reverberated softly around the room.

"I'll drink to that," she said. The last year had been the worst in her life. There was only one thing stopping it from getting any better: the man who had stalked her throughout.

* * * *

Max kept thinking about what Talia had been through and what was happening. She'd given up her life to care for her nephew. Leaving the work she'd adored behind had taken great courage. As if that wasn't enough to deal with she had her jerk of a brother-in-law.

"I don't know what to do about Roy," she said as she sipped at the wine, her shoulders slumping.

Should he tell her? Might it make her feel safer? "I have a friend watching the house," he finally said.

"You do? Who?" she asked with a look of surprise on her face.

"His name is Fireball. He owns a security firm with another man named Geekie, and he deals with some of the safety at the hangar where I've been working these past few days."

"You need security?"

"Sometimes the work I do is top secret," Max said.

"Really?" Talia looked at him wide-eyed, and he nodded. "Do you think having someone watch the house is warranted?"

He frowned. "You don't? Jeez, Talia, Roy is stalking the hell out of you, and he's becoming dangerous, which means he's escalating out of control."

Her shoulders slumped and now he wished he'd said nothing, but she needed to be aware of what was going on, and if that frightened her, it meant she'd be extra vigilant. However, he had no intention of letting her or Charlie out of sight. She wasn't due back to work for a few days, so they'd both be home. If she hadn't had this time off, he would have had no end to worry about them both.

She fiddled with a strand of her hair, and even that turned him on. He took the glass from her, setting them both on the small table.

"Come here," he said, opening his arms.

For a moment, she hesitated but not for long before she did as he asked. Max caged her so she was tightly close to him, her head under his chin. The scent from her hair was fresh, and summery and made him think of coconuts—the same as when he bumped into her for the first time.

He waited for her to speak. She was quiet and he didn't want to spoil the moment, but after about ten minutes of silence he wondered if she'd fallen asleep.

"Hey," he whispered in her ear.

"Umm," she murmured.

"I thought you were asleep," he said.

"No, just nicely comfortable."

"Good."

She leaned her head back a little, and his attention was on her mouth. He teased his lips over hers before setting small, tender kisses along her cheekbone to the lobe of her ear where he nibbled the soft skin.

"Are you involved with anyone back home?"

"Do you think I'm the type of man to be dating

someone and then sit here with you in my arms?"

She jolted upright, her shoulders straight and stiff. "No, of course not, but I felt it was something I should ask. I'm sorry. I should have known you wouldn't be like that."

Max hesitated before speaking. "Talia?"

She was pale, but that was nothing new—she had that kind of creamy English completion—and her eyes looked confused. It was as if she wasn't used to being in this situation with a man.

Reaching for her hand and turning it palm up, he kissed it. "Honey, you don't have to hide anything from me."

"I have a lot of responsibility," she said.

"I know that."

"It's not just Charlie and me. I'm responsible for my sister as well."

"What are you trying to tell me?" He let go of her and frowned as he looked at her.

She clasped her hands together tightly. "It's a lot to deal with, and it takes up nearly all of my time." Her shoulders tensed, and she kept looking down at her hands.

"Not much time for you, is there?"

"No, but that's okay. I'm not complaining. I want to clarify the situation before anything happens between us." Her skittish gaze jumped to his. "I haven't had much experience with men," she said, a blush appearing on her face. "And I suppose no one ever attracted me that much…until you."

Satisfaction warmed him and extended the protectiveness he already felt for her. His heart was drumming against his ribs, and without thought, he pushed her down onto the sofa so that she could not lift her legs. She giggled, and his doubts about being so forward with her vanished.

"Don't be nervous with me," he said, detecting a slight hesitation in her smile.

"I'm not," she declared. "But I am…a little out of practice." Her nose wrinkled in a cute kinda way.

"I've thought about you every single day since that first meeting. You're so soft and incredibly sexy."

"I feel a bit awkward."

Max hesitated; that wasn't what he wanted at all.

She must have seen the look on his face, because she added, "I don't mean I feel awkward with you. I feel awkward that I may have forgotten what to do."

He relaxed. *Thank God!*

"Talia." Her eyes looked straight into his. "We don't have to do anything you're not comfortable doing. We have all the time in the world. I'm happy being here with you."

She nodded.

"You're going through some really tough times with your sister and Charlie, not to mention what's happening with Roy."

Max tried not to squash her when she wrapped her arms around his neck and pulled him close. "I want you, Max, despite everything going on."

Oh, Lord.

"How light of a sleeper is Charlie?"

"He's like the dead once he's closed his eyes. It used to scare the crap out of me, and many a night I checked to make sure he was still breathing."

"How about we take this upstairs and see where it leads?"

"Do you want to?"

"Hell yes," he said, getting up and pulling Talia to her feet. He paused just long enough to kiss her. "Let's go and see if we can do something about relaxing you."

A powerful force passed between them—a wild, sexual heat.

She was tense despite her brave face, and he would work on that. Max hadn't been in a relationship for a long time. He'd had the occasional one-nighter and a few dates but nothing substantial. He had a funny feeling that this woman and her boy would become more than he'd ever thought two people would become in his life.

It didn't worry him; he'd always been an easy going guy who took life as it came, and although he worked tremendously hard he knew it wasn't the be-all and end-all of life.

Chapter 8

Talia led the way, although Max had hold of her hand, and as they reached the top of the stairs, the hallway had a golden glow from a plug-in night light. Not that Charlie ever got up, but she felt better knowing that he wouldn't be frightened of the dark if he ever did.

She stepped into her bedroom, opposite Charlie's, and switched on the light. Max shut the door behind them, still keeping hold of her hand.

The scent of roses and coconut was faint from the candle she had lit last night. Everything was tidy, from the soft floral bedspread to the matching cushions. Of course, none of the furniture was hers; she was waiting to settle down somewhere before she invested in items that would be difficult to move around like they'd been doing for the past year.

Talia was nervous. Sex had never been at the top of her priorities, but Max was unique and he seemed to think she was as well, which made her feel good.

Max drew her closer to him and stroked her cheek with his finger, and she smiled at him, leaning into his touch. Every beat of her heart reminded her of how close they had become in such a short time.

"Are you all right?" he asked, looking slightly worried, probably because she hadn't said a word since they entered her room.

"Yes." She tilted her head to look up at him under

her eyelashes. Biting her bottom lip, she took a small step backward, pulled her top over her head, and let it fall to the floor. She stood before him in a plain white bra and her work trousers.

"Holy hell, Talia. Just when I think I know you, you go and do something like that." His voice was low, and there was a slight flush high on his sharp cheekbones, his Adam's apple bobbing as if he was having trouble swallowing.

Talia smiled shyly as his eyes looked over her almost naked top half. There was something very empowering about having someone look at you in the way Max was. He moved toward her, slipping his hand onto her waist and drawing her close. His other hand trailed down her arm, giving her goosebumps as his fingertips smoothed her skin to cup the back of her neck.

"Beautiful," he whispered.

He kissed her jaw, then moved on to nibble at her earlobe. She couldn't stop the moan that came from deep inside her. She tilted her head to give him more access as he caressed her neck down to the dip of her shoulder that was oh-so-sensitive.

Max used his teeth to make little love-bite kisses while she laid her hands on his chest before moving them around his neck. She threaded her fingers into his hair and pulled tightly. An ocean of pleasure coming in waves of potent desire gripped her.

Talia could feel her nipples tightening; she needed his mouth there, and her hands were continually pushing him in the hope that he would get the hint. But Max was taking it slow, almost painfully, and she needed him to touch her where she was desperate for it. God, she was so close and he still had his clothes on. She was never going to last. How embarrassing.

"Hey," he said. "Tell me what's going on." He looked at her, and his eyes were darker than she'd ever seen them.

"Oh, God." She leaned her forehead on his.

"Do you want to stop?" he asked gently.

"No." She shook her head…God, she didn't. "It's been a long time for me."

He closed his eyes for a second, and when he opened them they were so dark that they'd almost turned black. It slightly elevated his breath as he looked back at her.

"How long is *long*?"

"Over two years." But she didn't tell him that it had been nothing special.

"How can that be?" he asked in a throaty tone. "I only have to look at you and I'm turned on."

"You are?" she asked, surprised by that minor revelation.

"Oh, yes…you have no idea," he said as he slowly walked her back toward the bed, looking straight into her eyes. "Let's take this slow."

Slow…slow…I can't last that long!

Lust burned through her veins in a scarlet web of desire. She'd never felt so powerless; the urgency seemed to have taken over her body. It was as if his body teased her with a promise of what was to come.

His fingers found the button to her trousers as he trailed a hand down her naked skin from shoulder to waist Max unfastened it and drew the zipper down, she felt the whispering touch of his fingers against her skin.

All the while he kept his eyes on hers, a carnal desire overwhelmingly blatant in his gaze.

Talia gave him a helping hand, pushing her trousers

down and stepping out of them so that she stood in front of him in her plain, white cotton. Oh, how she wished she had some sexy lingerie on instead of what she'd put on that morning. But judging by the look on his face, it didn't make one iota of difference.

"Talia, you are beautiful," he said in a deep, throaty voice.

She reached for the buttons on his shirt, unfastening them slowly because her fingers were shaking so much. She could feel the hair on his torso against her knuckles as she made it to the very last one. Slipping his shirt off and down his arms, she let it drop to the floor before allowing her eyes to feast on his body. She was not disappointed; he was all hot-hard and exquisitely formed.

Max drew her to him; it wasn't gentle, but she didn't feel that way either. She was so ready for him that if he didn't do something soon… His mouth totally destroyed any shyness she was feeling. Lingering lips ravished the skin on her neck as open-mouthed, hot, wet kisses took her breath away.

When his tongue traced the curve of her breast she wanted to rip off her bra. They must have been thinking the same thing, because by the time the thought entered her mind his fingers had nimbly undone the clasp, and he let the straps fall down her arms to the floor.

Max stood back for a moment, concentrating on her painful nipples, making them tent to a rigid desire. He leaned down and kissed her, his lips opening her mouth as his tongue did wonderful things to hers.

From the very core of her body, she felt the tingling, the need to push hard into him, which was so overpowering. She took his hand and leaned it against the wetness of her panties. The ache between her thighs grew more and more insistent.

He groaned loudly, letting his head fall against her shoulder. "Holy hell, Talia…you're so wet."

"I can't wait, I'm sorry," she said as the embarrassment she had felt left with any shyness she'd had.

"Don't be sorry. My God, you're so sexy," he said as he touched her through the material, the hungry waves of desire coming in an undulation sweep of passion.

When he moved his hand she felt trapped between torment and ecstasy and couldn't stop the hiss of breath, a sound that was half-pain, half-pleasure. He took her shoulders, lowering her down to the mattress before pushing her back. He hooked his thumbs under the elastic, drawing her panties down her legs and over her ankles.

"Let's see what we can do about making you more comfortable," he said as her head swam in a tidal wave of emotions.

* * * *

As Max lay over Talia, he still had his pants on, which was where they would stay…for now. He wanted to watch her come with his hand first. Max almost spontaneously combusted when she took off her top and saw her white bra. Never in a million years would he have thought that would be a turn-on. Erotic oblivion nearly overtook him when he saw how perfect her dusky rose nipples were, pebbled and tight.

He'd been surprised at her boldness, making his desire to go into overdrive. . He discovered that the periphery of his vision was completely erased, leaving him solely focused on what was in front of him—a beautiful, sexy woman who had no idea how much she drove him insane.

His body was on fire, but he wanted to hold out as long as he could and concentrate on giving her what she needed...several times. Max moved to her side, and she gave a muted sound of disappointment.

"Hey," he said. "Are you okay?"

"Yes...no...yes." Talia took his hand, showing him what she wanted, he felt with his fingers her wet sex and he couldn't stop the moan that erupted from his chest. She had totally shocked him in so many ways tonight. One minute she'd been shy the next so forward that it had been like a different woman.

Lust burned in his brain, and he couldn't think of anything else but pleasing her. She squirmed against him, her body shaking, and heat streaked through him as he felt how desperately close she was. He leaned down and traced her nipple with his tongue.

"Max," she whispered, her voice raw and wild.

As her body lifted off the mattress he used his hand on her tummy to steady her. She took hold of his fingers and persuaded them to touch her sex. His hand covered the damp curls, and he moaned deep in his throat as the feel of her arousal spread over his fingers.

Her hips started to rock against his hand, and he worked his fingers into the wetness as his thumb parted the wet folds of her labia. He blew against her nipple before sucking softly at the hardened flesh, licking and nibbling as he drank in her sexiness.

Her sensuality was honest, and made the blood pump through his veins, his heart throbbing at a manic pace. His fingers drenched with her need, and she'd started to rock into his hand, her slim hips lifting off the mattress as she tried to get him to push harder into her. Faster, more urgent with each thrust of his hand. He could smell her need, and he was dying to taste her. Max kissed his way over to her other breast, flicking the tip of her nipple with his tongue.

It was almost impossible to hold back, but he did, inhibiting his need so she could enjoy hers. Max sensed how close she was. And then she went taut with the release. For a moment, he was stunned and didn't move, just letting her ride out the urgent hunger that had captivated her body as he buried his fingers deep inside her, the palm of his hand pressed hard against the nub of tiny nerves.

She couldn't have hidden her pleasure even if she had tried. It was evident in her expression and her throaty cries. It seemed like forever before her body started to loosen and become limp. God, he couldn't stop looking at her. He'd never seen anything like the power of desire that had gone through her body. There was a blush on her cheeks, although he wasn't sure if that was from passion or shyness. He saw both when he took her arm that she had thrown over her eyes.

"I'm sorry," she said in a shy whisper.

"What for?"

"For not waiting."

"Oh, Talia," he said, his voice low. "You have no idea how stunning you looked. I was happy enough to let you go where you wanted."

He leaned down and kissed her, softly to begin with and then full-on, unadulterated passion-infused, animalistic hunger. He felt a shudder go through her body, and then she pushed him back.

"One of us is wearing too many clothes," she said.

"And that would be me."

He crawled off her, shucked his trousers and boxers to the floor, and fished out a condom from his wallet. Slipping it on, he watched her as she stared back at him. *Fuck,* she was going to set him alight with the glow of fire coming from her eyes. He stretched out beside her, and she trailed her hand down his abdomen. He grabbed it, brought it to his mouth, and kissed it.

She frowned. "Don't you want me to touch you?"

"Honey, I'm on a ragged edge here. I can barely think as it is."

"Oh." Her frown smoothed out and she smiled. "Okay, let's do something about that."

"My sentiments exactly," he said.

Done talking, Max took a moment to play with her breasts before easing her into a kiss that was urgent with need. He loved how her lips felt against his; they were so honest, displaying all the heat and passion she felt.

Max explored her heat with his fingers. She was wet...wet from coming and wet from desire. He knew Tallis would feel sensitive there after her orgasm, so he kept it light, his fingers quickly moving against the wetness. It was seconds before she threw her head back into the pillows, gasping.

Her eyes were closed, and he wanted them open so he could see her every emotion. "Talia, look at me."

She lifted her long, dark lashes, and her honey-colored eyes gazed back at him. He reached down between their bodies and climbed over her, positioning himself before slowly easing inside her.

Fuck...she's snug. Max was shaking as she stretched and melted around him, and for a moment, he stayed still, enjoying the raw need inside him.

Her hand cupped his jaw, and her fingers brushed his beard. Her gaze caressed him in such a way that he knew it wasn't just one night he saw in those eyes and she was all he wanted, all he could think about like an endless dream.

Groaning, Max gave in to his need for her. He covered her mouth with his own, their lips carnal as their mouths mated, teeth and tongues savage with desire. He opened his hand onto her hip, touching the soft flesh as he guided her into a rhythmic movement that soon became urgent.

As each thrust became faster and more insistent,, their breaths mingled with potent intensity, and he braced his forearms on either side of her. More profound, faster, as all reasoning fled, leaving only the madness of desire. She wrapped her slim legs around him, gasping louder with every movement of his body.

Her arms held on tighter as he rode her harder than he thought possible. She groaned as their slick bodies moved against each other, setting fire to the all-consuming, raw need. Suddenly, she stiffened and cried out. That was all he needed to tip him over the edge. He gathered her close as an almighty reverberating release happened that had him shaking in the most powerful orgasm he'd ever experienced.

* * * *

Talia felt the haze of pleasure, her body deliciously sore and satisfied in the blissful afterglow, one she didn't even know existed. Max's heavy weight was comforting as she lightly scraped her short nails up and down his damp back. Loving it, she hugged him.

Sex had never been like that before. If it had, she might have done it more often. Talia held onto him as his muscles started to relax; like hers, his breathing slowed down. He kissed her gently. His gaze lingered on her face, and his fingers smoothed her hair away from her forehead before leaning in to kiss the moist skin. When he went to move, she held onto him, and he looked at her.

"Don't," she said. "Just for a few moments. I like the feel of you on top of me."

Max kissed her shoulder, smiling as he came up onto his elbows. "I'm not too heavy?"

She shook her head. "No."

"What are you thinking?"

"That you are good."

"No...*we* were good." His eyes blazed with emotion.

"I always found it hard to achieve pleasure from sex."

"Really?" He looked shocked, but then a smile spread across his face. "Honey, you came twice, and trust me, you were enjoying it."

She grinned and couldn't believe they were talking about sex as if it was an everyday conversation. That was the joy she felt with Max. Just being next to Max made her so relaxed.

"I'm sorry I'm not more experienced," she said, feeling like a gawky teenager.

"Hey, you were wonderful, and I wanted this to be about you. And let's face it; I think you could tell that I loved every moment of our lovemaking," Max murmured as those warm, sexy lips kissed the bridge of her nose, making her feel more than she should have.

Trying to convince herself that it was only one night and he wouldn't be there forever, she decided she would enjoy whatever came her way.

But wasn't that going to be hard on Charlie? Talia saw that the little boy had already built a relationship with Max. Jeez, life throws some heck of a curveball sometimes.

"What's with the frown?" Max asked, and the feel of his lips on her forehead seemed to dissipate every worry she had.

"Why me?"

"What do you mean?" He lifted himself off her and leaned on his elbow, watching her.

"Well, I'm not a beauty, and I have Charlie."

"Talia, you underestimate your beauty—both inside and out—and surely you can see how I feel about Charlie?"

"You are fabulous with him."

"Tell me why you would even think that about yourself?"

Perhaps she shouldn't have started this conversation now because suddenly she felt very naked and under scrutiny. "Tilly was always the one that everyone gravitated towards. She was pretty, funny, and had a style that screamed *look at me*. Even now, after the accident, her face is stunning." She glanced at him, and affection glowed in his eyes. That wasn't what she had expected to see. Pity, yes, but not affection.

"So, Tilly was an actress?"

Talia nodded.

"How did she manage to marry such a scumbag?"

As she looked at Max, it was hard for Talia to see anything else. They were soft and gentle as he spoke to her, and she felt her heart melt. Wow, this man was getting into every crevice of her soul and more.

"We all knew what he was like, but at that time, Tilly thought he was the bee's knees, and she was already pregnant with Charlie by then." She shook her head at her sister's stupidity. "Tilly had already married him in a drunken haze. We were all shocked, especially Mum and Dad. They were heartbroken. Tilly was…well, she was their favorite," she said, recalling how many times she had been made to feel far less important than her sister. "Anyway, it took her a few months and several black eyes to realize he wasn't the one for her." She bit down on her lip. "With the number of times Roy hit Tilly,, I'm surprised Charlie wasn't born with something wrong with him. Mum and Dad loved their grandson and were so proud of her achievements as an actress."

"They must have been proud of you as well. Hell, you have a doctorate in archaeology. That's not an easy thing to achieve."

Talia blushed at his praise. "They were proud of me, but not as much as Tilly." She placed both her hands beneath her cheek. "Tell me about you?"

He breathed in deeply, lay down on his back, and looked up at the ceiling. "Not much to tell really. My mom died giving birth to me and my dad did the best he could as the only parent."

"But?" she asked, sensing that there was more.

"But he was an inventor, and not a very successful one. He worked at a grocery store during the day and invented in the basement at night."

"What was he like?"

Max smiled as if remembering. "Have you ever seen a caricature of a mad scientist?"

She nodded, smiling.

"I guess that was my dad. He worked on unlikely

ways to save the world with inventions that never seemed to work," he laughed. "Dad tended to live in the eccentricity of his creations."

"It must have been hard for you."

"Not really. It was what I was used to." She felt sad for him.

All of a sudden, he lifted her on top of him. She squealed as she landed with her core,, feeling his very hard sex. Almost immediately, she was wet and ready, and the ache between her thighs grew increasingly insistent.

"I can think of better things to do than talk," he said as he drew her down to put a rigid nipple into his mouth.

She couldn't agree more as she closed her eyes and let her body succumb to the pleasure she knew was on the horizon.

* * * *

Max awoke, lifting his arm to see the time. A little after seven, the darkness peeped in through a gap in the drapes. A flood of memories from last night enveloped him, and he turned to see that the space beside him was empty.

Last night Talia had curled herself around him, her silky legs tangled with his, and he'd felt her even breathe against his chest as she fell asleep. Max had never before felt so comfortable with a woman and had never been a cuddler, but with her it was…nice. And now he was missing it.

Sitting up, he fumbled to find the switch to the lamp on the nightstand. The flood of light made him wince a little until he got used to it. He looked around the room and saw everything was tidy and neat; she'd even picked up his clothes and laid them over a chair in the corner.

Flicking the quilt back, he swung his legs to the floor and headed to the en-suite. When he came out, he dressed while remembering last night, and damned if he didn't feel himself getting hard. They'd made love twice and she'd climaxed four times. He could still smell her heady scent of her and hear the sounds she made as she enjoyed her pleasure.

It had made him feel good to know he had brought her so much enjoyment, but it wasn't one-sided. He couldn't remember the last time he'd orgasmed so hard and long. Fuck, it had been good; more than good…fantastic. Talia made him feel like a teenager, but with more experience.

Damn, but that was crazy; he'd only known her a few weeks.

He opened the bedroom door and voices drifted up the stairs. Max followed the sounds to the kitchen and pushed the door open. For a moment, he watched the two people who made his heart feel warm and contented.

They were sitting at the kitchen table, filled with empty toilet rolls, cotton wool, laughter, and glitter. He saw a more relaxed Talia than he'd seen before. Even though it was so early, they seemed to be having a good time… Wasn't this how Christmas was supposed to be?

He noticed that the dark circles under her eyes, which had been evident before, were gone. The laughter reached her eyes, and that made him feel happy.

She looked up at him and smiled. "Hey."

Charlie turned around. "Max, you're up. Aunty Tally wouldn't let me wake you, and I wanted you to help."

"Contrary to your beliefs, Charlie, not everyone wants to get up before eight to make Christmas decorations."

Max laughed at the sheer shock on the little boy's face at Talia's words. "I've never made decorations at any time of day, but I'd like to learn," Max said.

"Really?" Charlie said. "Didn't your mum and dad teach you?"

"No."

"My mum didn't like all the mess," Charlie said, looking sad for a moment, and then he grinned. "Aunty Tally is a good teacher," he said, holding the glue pot, surrounded by his sticky fingers, and glitter everywhere.

"I bet she is," Max said, his eyes on her. She had tight jeans and a Christmas jumper in red and white that said jingle all the way and had small bells attached. He loved the way she blushed, it turned him on big time.

"Coffee?" she asked him, pushing her chair back to stand up.

Gently but firmly, he nudged her back into her seat. "You carry on with what you're doing, and I'll make us both a cup."

"That would be nice. Thank you." She told him where everything was.

He spooned the instant into the mugs. He took it black but he'd seen Talia make hers and he knew she added milk and sugar. While he watched the two of them, he folded his arms and leaned back on the countertop. To be honest, he wasn't sure who was having the most fun.

When the water had boiled he filled both cups and set them on the table before sitting down to join them.

"Max, do you like my jumper?" Charlie asked as he stood up so Max could see the snowman with cotton wool snow all over it.

"I love it," he said.

"You're brave," Talia said to him, grinning. "It's at your own risk that you sit there. I can't guarantee that you won't get covered in glitter."

"I'm brave too," Charlie piped up.

"Why are you brave?" Max asked him.

"Because I helped Aunty Tally get wood from the garden so we could start the fire. She said we had to be really careful because it was still dark."

"Aunty Tally shouldn't be out on her own," he said, narrowing his eyes at her.

"She wasn't on her own," Charlie said indignantly. "I was with her. I'm a Power Ranger and can protect her from anything."

He caught the anxiety in her glance at him.

"I don't know what a Power Ranger is, bud, but I'm sure glad you went with her."

Charlie then went on to tell him about the Tyrannosaurus power he had, and although it was barely eight AM they all sat around the table and made decorations. Max had never known anyone who talked as much as Charlie did.

They were like a family.

When they finished, Talia put the decoration on a tray to take into the front room.

"Okay, Charlie, where are we putting all of these?" she asked him.

"Aunty Tally, I'm a little tired. Would you mind doing it for me?" he asked as he sat on the sofa and folded his arms. "Max will help you."

Max laughed. "I think we've had our orders."

"It seems so," she said, smiling at her nephew.

At that moment, Molly jumped up on Charlie's lap, settling herself down for a nap. "And now I can't move," he said, pointing at his lap.

"It seems you're both sleepy," Talia said as she started to hang the decorations they'd made.

"Hey, guess what, Max?"

"What's that, bud?"

"Not only is Santa coming tonight, but it's my birthday tomorrow and I'm six."

"Wow, you're almost a man."

Charlie giggled. "Don't be silly."

"We have a lot to do today. We have to do the last-minute shopping, and we're going to see Mummy later," Talia said gently to her nephew.

"I've made Mummy a card, but I know she won't understand it," the little boy said sadly.

"Aww, honey." Talia sat down beside Charlie, putting her arm around him. "Mummy will know it's from you. She may not show it, because she can't express her emotions as we do, but they are still there inside of her and she's going to love what you have for her. Okay?"

He nodded. "It's okay, Aunty Tally, I understand," he said, smiling up at her.

Talia hugged him before getting back up to help Max with the decorations, and he couldn't help but notice the tears shimmering in her eyes.

Max drew in a breath as he handed Talia the scotch tape so she could stick the colored chain to the mantel above the fire. "I have some shopping I need to do," he said. "So I can take you in the car."

Talia turned from hanging the last of the cotton wool Santas. "Are you sure?"

He nodded and he thought he saw relief in her eyes.

"Are you going to marry my Aunty Tally?"

Max almost choked, and the horror on Talia's face as she slapped a hand over her mouth almost made him grin.

"What makes you say that, Charlie?" he asked, almost afraid of what might come out of his mouth.

"Cause when I came to get Aunty Tally up, I saw you in her bed, and that only happens if you're going to get married. My friend Dan told me so."

" Charlie—" Talia quickly finding her tongue interrupted Max from answering.

"Don't be so silly, honey. We hardly know Max."

"Well, why was he in your bed, then?"

An innocent question from a six-year-old, and he couldn't help but chuckle. The word "marry" didn't bother Max in the least.

Talia scowled at him, probably because he was chuckling. He couldn't wait to hear her explanation.

"Max was sharing because he is far too big for the sofa." She slipped him a warning glance.

Oh yeah, that should do it. Max could see the cogs ticking over in the young boy's mind.

"You could sleep with me, but my bed is small. I'll be getting a bigger one soon. My legs are getting really long." He lifted one up for Max to see, knocking poor Molly off his knee.

"Wow," Max said, "they are getting long."

Relief showed in Talia's eyes, and just like that, Charlie had forgotten what he'd initially asked.

Max leaned down, whispering into Talia's ear, "Out of the mouths of babes." He winked at her, and she dug her elbow into his ribs.

Yep, he was going to marry this girl.

Chapter 9

Talia was doing some last-minute shopping, while Max had taken Charlie with him. It was nice to have someone to share the responsibilities, but she had to remember that Max would go home soon, and she would be on her own again. April had rung her while they were in the car and she had arranged to meet her for coffee.

After making sure Max knew where she would be, Talia sat down, ordering a pumpkin spice cappuccino and mint tea for her friend.

Her conversation with Charlie from earlier in the day returned to her, and she placed her cold hands on her face, hoping to cool down her hot cheeks. MARRY- The word still echoed in her ears

When her nephew had walked into her room this morning at an unusually early hour, which she could only put down to his excitement for the time of year, Talia nearly had a heart attack. She worried about what kind of effect it would have on Charlie. But he didn't seem bothered by the noise coming from his bedroom.

God, what must Max have thought? Although, thinking about it, he hadn't seemed bothered at all. In fact, Max seemed to find the complete debacle amusing. Talia thought he might have made some excuse to leave them, but he didn't.

"And what is making those cheeks so red?" April hugged her before sitting down. Immediately, she dipped her tea bag in and out of the cup. "So, are you okay?"

"Yes, I'm good, thanks. Look at you. Jeez, April, that baby is ready to come out."

"Tell me about it. Every organ in my body is squished together, and my bladder is taking a front seat." Taking a sip of her drink, April screwed her face up and leaned toward Talia, sniffing her coffee. "I can't wait to get some caffeine inside me."

Talia laughed. "I take it you're ready to get rid of the tummy?"

"You better believe it. I feel like an elephant."

"April, you look beautiful."

"Ha, you are looking through rose-colored glasses."

She smiled at her as she took a big bite of the large cream donut Talia had purchased for her.

"Yum, yum, " April closed her eyes and Talia giggled.

"Your laughing. This cake is the nearest thing to sex currently. Steve treats me like I need to be wrapped in cotton wool," she said of her husband."

"April, he's just looking after you."

"I know he is, and I love him all the more for it. But this is why I need the cake."

Talia raised her eyebrows.

"Sex but in eating form."

She pressed her hand to her mouth to stifle the giggle.

"So," April asked "What has been going on with Roy?

Talia filled her in on the events of the last few days.

"He's escalating, Talia. I'm frightened for you."

Talia shoved her hair back in a frustrated gesture. "I'm not moving again. Every time I do I'm giving into him."

"I know, honey, but he's getting dangerous. Have you reported him to the police?"

"On numerous occasions, but I can't prove anything, and until I do, they're not interested."

"Why don't you and Charlie come stay with me? Just over the holidays?"

"And put you in danger? Absolutely not." Talia bit her lip. "I have someone staying with me."

April looked at her in surprise, and then her face lit up and she grinned at Talia. "Oh my God, it's a man?"

Talia's face heated up. Damn blushing, it was such a nuisance at her age. She nodded. "Yes." Picking her cup up, she sipped at the frothy liquid, enjoying the spicy flavor.

"How come I haven't heard about this? Tell me more."

"Because it's only just happened, and I'm not certain that it's anything at all," she said, not really sure what was happening between the two or that there was a thing. Joy bubbled up inside her as the events from last night with him completely overwhelmed her, it was surreal.

"Talia, honey…as much as I want you to be happy, please be careful."

"You know I am." She smiled at April. Although she had only drunk coffee, she felt drunk with happiness. God, she hoped it would never end. "Max is an aerospace engineer from America." Her heart did that leaping thing, even at the sound of his name on her lips.

"Holy cow, Talia…you're in love."

Was she?

Warmth filled her chest. *Bloody hell*…she just

might be.

"I'm so happy for you. You deserve it. Tell me everything." April winked at her. "And I mean everything."

They spent the next half hour talking. April was always able to put things into perspective.

"I'm so glad Max was there, Talia."

Last night she'd felt numb all over as she'd watched her shed burnt to the ground. It had shattered her and left her skin crawling with fear. If it hadn't been for Max, the despair would have dragged her down and she would have crumbled inside.

After the year Talia had just been through, she wasn't sure if she would have been able to pick herself up from the emotional depression that would have disintegrated any fight she had left. But the thought of Charlie and how he needed her so much.

Her nephew was the driving force behind her perseverance. And Max had been there to hold her up, to make her feel like she wasn't alone…for the season.

She placed her hand over her heart and said, "He's so good with Charlie. I trust him, April. I don't know what will happen when he's due to go home, but I'll cross that bridge when we come to it." She sighed as she settled her hand on the table, palm up. "Charlie and I deserve some happiness?"

April laid her hand over Talia's. "You do, you really do." She frowned as if trying to find the right words. "You know where I am, anytime day or night."

Talia gripped her fingers, smiling at her. "I know, and thank you for being my friend."

"Hey, you remember when I met Steve, and what a mess I was?"

Talia nodded.

"You were there for me. That's what friends do for each other."

She inhaled as tears settled behind her lashes. God, she was an emotional wreck at the moment.

"Don't you start or you'll set me off, and believe me, you do not want to see this pregnant lady cry."

It did what April had intended, making them both laugh.

"Aunty Tally, Aunty April." Charlie threw himself into April's waiting arms.

"Hey there. Jeez, Charlie, you need to stop growing, I can't fit you on my knee anymore."

Charlie stood back from being squeezed tightly and looked her up and down. "That's because you have a big baby in your tummy."

April giggled happily. "You're right, honey, I do."

A new voice intruded into the conversation. "Hey, are you okay?"

Talia was the target of the question. Max's caring voice filled her with joy.

Talia looked up at him and nodded. "I'm fine, thank you." He made her quiver from head to toe, which did nothing to help with her heated complexion. "Max, this is my best friend, April."

"So, Max, you're the one making her blush at the slightest mention of your name."

Appalled at her friend's bluntness, she stood up as April took Max's hand in a gesture of friendliness.

"Nice to meet you," he said.

"Are you going to be looking after Talia? 'Cause if you hurt her…."

Oh God, this was worse than taking your first

boyfriend home to meet your parents.

"I will be looking after both of them, you needn't worry about a thing," Max said with a slow smile as he moved to stand beside Talia, letting his arm fall around her waist.

Talia looked up at him with an incredulous dazed look that she couldn't help.

"We've got lots of shopping," Charlie said, breaking the silence.

Talia looked at him; he had a few shopping bags in his hand. "Wow, you have been busy." Was that her breathless voice?

"We have secrets," Charlie said, putting his finger to his lips. "Max told me that it's a secret."

"Just between us, bud," he said to the boy with a smile.

"Okay," April said. "This exhausted, pregnant girl needs to get home, and it looks like snow. I hate driving in it."

Talia moved and she felt bereft at the loss of Max's warmth. She went and hugged April. "You let me know the minute that baby comes."

"I will," she said. "I love his accent…I like him," she whispered in Talia's ear.

Talia smiled at her as she drew away. "Here are your gifts," she said, handing April the bag she'd had beside her.

"And this is your birthday gift," April said, passing Charlie a big parcel.

With a wide grin and eyes that sparkled Charlie gave his bags to Max before hugging the wrapped gift. "Thank you," he said in an excited voice.

They all said their goodbyes, then Talia, Max, and

Charlie—who wouldn't let go of his gift—walked to the multi-story parking lot.

"You don't have to take us to the care home. I would completely understand if you didn't want to." And she would. It wasn't something she looked forward to…it tore at her heart each time she went. Her once vivacious sister didn't even recognize her now.

"Good or bad, I'm here for you," Max said as he drove with expertise in the weather that was not the best. They'd already had so much snow this year that she was surprised when more flakes started hitting the windscreen. "All you need to do is direct me," he said, glancing at her as he stopped at a traffic light.

She told him the address, which he put into the navigation system.

"You and I…we are now in a relationship," he told her.

For a moment, she felt stymied by those words. "We are?"

"Oh yes, honey, we are."

She opened her mouth to say something, but nothing came out. Max reached over and, taking her hand, he brought it up to his lips and kissed it before setting it back on her lap.

Talia turned her head to see that Charlie had fallen asleep, his lashes resting on his cheeks, his hands beneath his head. Despite being on his booster cushion, he looked as comfy and relaxed as if he was lying on his bed.

She was overwhelmed by her emotions and thoughts, and she lost track of Roy's threats.

She loved it. Max had made such a difference in their lives in a very short time.

But Roy was never far away from her thoughts even when she tried to forget him. Closing her eyes, she wished that part of her life would disappear. Charlie's dad held a grudge against her, and she knew he'd do anything to get back at her.

"We're here," Max said, and she sat up and breathed in for a second before exhaling.

"You can—" she started saying before Max cut her off.

He narrowed his eyes. "I'm coming with you, Talia. We've already had this talk. Unless you'd rather I didn't?"

She raised her chin and gazed at him. "I'd rather you did," she replied.

Max nodded, and before she could step out, he had gotten out of the car and opened the door for her.

Taking his hand, she exited the car, and he settled his arm around her.

"Okay?"

Talia nodded.

She took a moment to scan her surroundings, as she always did, but there was no sign of Roy. But she knew there was no way he had just disappeared. She was sure the fire had been a warning of something more to come. How or when that would happen, she had no idea. But for the moment she felt protected and secure having this man beside her.

* * * *

Max wanted nothing more than to protect Talia and Charlie. It didn't help that he had a terrible feeling about things, but he kept that to himself. He still had security watching them and had spoken to Fireball that morning.

It seemed that Roy had spent some time inside for

armed robbery and had a very nasty drug habit. Max had no illusions about what Roy would do, which was why he'd asked Fireball to keep the security measures in place.

Max reached into the back seat to unfasten Charlie's safety belt. "Hey, buddy, we're here," he said as the little boy opened his eyes and focused for a moment before he scampered out of the car.

He followed Max to the trunk.

Talia took the packages from Max and handed Charlie the card he'd made. "Here you go," she said. "Put your hat on."

He took it from his pocket and slipped it on over his hair. It was a little lopsided, but it would protect him from the falling snow.

Max wanted to draw them both into his arms that he had to hold back physically, and empathy gripped him hard. He knew from what Talia had said that she found these visits emotionally exhausting.

They left the car and Max followed them into the nursing home. He opened the glass door for them, and they entered a foyer. The warmth hit him, making his face sting a little bit.

Talia walked toward the sign-in desk as Charlie skipped ahead; he knew how to go. A giant Christmas tree was in the corner next to two gray sofas. Beneath the tree were many gifts Max assumed had been left for the staff.

"Hold on a minute, Charlie," Talia said as she smiled at the woman who greeted them.

"Hi there, Charlie. I haven't seen you in ages. Tell me, are you excited for Santa Claus?"

"I am, and it's my birthday tomorrow," he told the

woman who had on a purple uniform and a name tag that said *Moira*. Max estimated her age to be in her early fifties.

"It is? How old are you going to be?"

"Six," he said proudly.

Max watched the conversation between the two of them and smiled.

"How is she?" Talia asked the nurse.

"Could I have a word with you in private?"

Talia turned toward Max, a worried look in her eyes. "Do you want to stay here?" she asked.

"I don't mind. Would you like me to go with Charlie?"

Talia frowned as if she didn't know what to say.

Empathy took hold of him. "Hey," he said, grasping her hand and squeezing it. "I don't mind."

She was introspective for a moment, and then she nodded. "Okay, thank you."

He kept hold of her hand for a second before letting it go because Charlie was pulling on his other one.

"See you in a minute," she said. "Mummy is in her room, Charlie."

"Come on, Max. I know the way."

They walked down a carpeted hallway. From what he could tell, the artwork on the walls was created by some of the residents. It was all very colorful. Hanging from the ceiling were bright, shiny, seasonal decorations which seemed to be the theme to where Tilly was.

When they reached her room, the door was open. There was a large, adjustable bed with a cabinet at one side. Max recognized Tilly right away as Talia's sister. She was beautiful and looked peaceful despite all the machines around her.

151

Charlie stood by Max's side for a few moments before he moved over to the bed. Tilly was staring into space at nothing, and it was one of the most heartbreaking things Max had ever seen.

The bed was so tall that Charlie had to stand on the chair at the side of it and lean over, then he shyly showed his mother the card he'd made for her. He didn't seem to notice that she displayed no recognition in her face. It occurred to Max that life was cruel to have left this woman with such dilapidating injuries. What kind of life was that? Then he felt bad for thinking that way…any life at all was worth saving.

Talia appeared beside him, and she looked as if she'd been crying. She flashed him a brief smile before going over to the bed. Sitting on the side of it, she talked to her sister as though there was nothing wrong with her, and then she lifted Charlie to sit beside his mum.

Max felt like a voyeur, so he left and went to sit on the sofa he'd seen when they entered the nursing home. Taking his phone from his pocket, he checked his emails and messages. There were a lot of them. He addressed what he could and left the rest until he could get to his laptop.

One message that did interest him was from Fireball. *Hey, Max, just letting you know that there have been some developments. Can you ring asap?*

Max made his way outside and gave his friend a call.

* * * *

Talia tried to take in what Moira had said. Tilly had been steadily getting worse, and she had pneumonia…again. The nursing home had been about to call her to tell her that they didn't think she'd make it through the night. And they wanted to ensure that the

DNR she had signed for Tilly stood. It did.

Tears clouded her vision, even though she always left Tilly with the thought that it might be the last time she saw her sister alive. Charlie saw her through a child's eyes, which was good, and she was glad he had come with them today.

How did you explain to a six-year-old boy that his mummy was dying? The only compensation was that he had never spent much time with her. First, it had been her parents who cared for him, and Talia took on the role when they died.

As Charlie read his mother a story Talia saw Max in her peripheral vision, and she stood up and walked over to him.

Max put his arm around her and kissed her temple. "Is everything okay?"

"They don't think Tilly will last through the night."

"Aw, Tally," he said, using Charlie's name for her. "I'm so sorry."

"Yeah, me too. Why don't you go home? We're going to stay."

"I'd have a long way to go, and getting a flight over Christmas would be manic." He took hold of her hand as he drew her near and smoothed his thumb across her knuckles. "If you don't mind…I'll stay."

"I'll give you the keys." She started to leave him to get them from her handbag, but he held her tighter.

"No, I meant I'm staying here with you, if that's okay?"

Was that okay? God, she could have kissed him. And she did, on the jaw, his beard tickling her nose. "Yes, I'd love it if you stayed with us. Thank you."

Max stroked her hair. "Are you okay, honey?"

A slight noise made both of them turn their heads.

"Aunty Tally, Mummy's eyes are open."

Talia hurried over to the bed. Usually, when Tilly's eyes were open they were vacant, but Talia would swear that she saw recognition in them. Taking hold of Tilly's hand, she squeezed it. Talia sat on the side of the bed, because her legs were like jelly and just by looking at her sister, Talia recognized this was different.

She couldn't stop the tears that fell down her cheeks, then she felt Max behind her, his arm holding onto her and Charlie.

The little boy looked up at her. "Is Mummy going to heaven now?"

She'd had numerous conversations with Charlie about this happening, and now that it was, she hoped she'd prepared him enough for it.

"Yes, honey, she is."

"And she'll be able to walk in heaven?"

"Mummy will be able to walk, run, and laugh."

"She'll be happier than she is now. Don't cry, Aunty Tally. Mummy will finally be able to get out of this bed."

Aww damn! She loved this boy, and she was so very proud of him. He was only six years old, he put her to shame with his view of what was happening.

A little over an hour later, Tilly passed away.

* * * *

Max carried Charlie in from the car, and Talia followed him up the stairs. Laying him on the bed, Max stood back so she could take his clothes off and put his PJs on. He didn't wake at all as she tucked him in and smoothed his hair back from his face. He had taken his mum's death as if it had been a gift to him; not because he was glad, but because he saw it as a release to a better life for her. It was the most unselfish moment she had ever witnessed between mum and son.

Getting up, she turned around and saw that Max had left the room. Talia walked out the door, shutting it behind her. She headed downstairs, and when she reached the bottom, she stopped for a second, trying to get a handle on her emotions.

She went into the living room where Max had revived the fire and was sitting on the sofa. A bottle of opened Shiraz and two glasses were on the coffee table.

"Come here," he said, patting the seat beside him.

She did as she was told, and without thought she fell into his arms, sobbing her heart out. Despite being twins, Talia and Tilly had never been really close, but she felt her sister's loss deep in her heart. The wealth of sadness was almost unbearable, and it was a while before the tears stopped and weariness overtook. It was so comfortable in his arms that she couldn't stop her eyes from closing just for a few moments to regain her composure.

Talia opened her eyes, and for an instant she wondered where she was, then she remembered crying in Max's arms. She looked up at the clock on the mantelpiece to see that it was two AM...on Christmas morning, and she still had some wrapping left to do. There was no sign of Max. She pushed the cover to the side he must have laid over her.

She remembered his comforting words as she cried herself to sleep. Without a doubt, she had fallen in love with him. He made it so easy for that to happen. The man was amazingly sweet and kind. If she was a betting person, which she wasn't, she'd put ten pounds down that he couldn't wait to get home.

Standing up, she stared at the blazing fire. The milk, carrot, and mince pie that Charlie had left for Santa before they'd gone out last night was still on the floor by the Christmas tree. There was only her and Charlie now. All she had to do was sort out Roy.

She entered the kitchen and found Max sitting at the table wrapping gifts. He looked up as she entered the room.

"That was great timing, that was my last gift." He stood up. "Tea, coffee, or wine?"

She looked at his glass, which was nearly empty. "Wine," she said. "I think I'm going to need it. I still have some things to do."

"I'll help," he said. "Sit down." He poured a drink for her and topped his up.

"First I need to get the turkey in the oven," she said, going toward the fridge.

"Done," Max said. "I hope that was okay, but I saw it and guessed it was meant to be in the oven rather than the sink."

"You guessed rightly. Wow, you are one of those men who can put their hand to anything." She smiled as she picked up the glass and sipped the red liquid. Sighing, she took a seat at the table.

"All part of living on your own for the last fourteen years." His eyes searched hers. "How are you feeling?" he asked in a soft voice.

"I'm okay, thanks. It was sad that Tilly went, but I think Charlie was okay about it."

"Charlie was amazing, so understanding about the whole situation."

"Yeah, he was. We'd talked about it many times. I knew it was coming, and I wanted to prepare him as much as I could. I'm glad he decided to come last night. He must have had a sixth sense that something was happening because he didn't want to go the last few times." She would have hated if Charlie hadn't had a chance to say his goodbyes.

"You did a great job."

"Thanks. Right, I need to get my skates on or Santa won't be coming down the chimney," Talia said as she grabbed a roll of Christmas paper.

For the next hour, they worked together to wrap and tag the gifts. They set all the Christmas presents under the tree, and placed Charlie's birthday ones on the coffee table. What she loved the most was sharing all of this with Max. She forgot about the arrangements she'd have to make for a short time. And of course, there was still Roy to deal with.

Glancing at the clock, she saw that it was 3:30. It wouldn't be long before Charlie got up, leaving her with a few hours to get some sleep. Standing up, she reached her hand behind her neck to smooth her taut muscles.

Max stood up and came behind her, his hands massaging her shoulders, easing away the tension and stiffness. She dropped her head, allowing him to work his magic. The moan that came from her was one of gratitude and pleasure. God, he had good, strong fingers.

"Thank you for your help," she said. "I could never have gotten through the last few hours without you."

He turned her around, and his dark eyes searched hers. He smoothed his fingers down her cheek.

"I have a bit of good news for you." He frowned. "I'm not sure I should have put it quite like that."

She looked at him expectantly. "You do?"

"Roy was found dead this afternoon from a drug

overdose."

She was incredibly relieved, but she also felt somewhat sad about Roy. He was Charlie's dad...perhaps one day he would clean himself up and be able to meet the son he turned away.

His use of drugs was never going to end well."

"I know what you're saying, but there are some people in this world that you just can't help."

Talia nodded. It was the society they lived in; something had to change. She breathed freely without worry for the first time in nearly a year.

She looked up at Max. "Will you sleep with me?"

He nodded. "Come on, honey."

Chapter 10

Max watched Talia as she checked on Charlie and set Rudolph the reindeer stocking on the end of his bed.

Aunty and nephew had been through so much tonight, yet they'd both been strong enough to survive what must have been hell. He felt sad for the little boy who'd lost a mom, but he had a fantastic aunty to help him through life, and she was one hell of a woman.

Charlie was a lucky boy.

She shut her nephew's door before turning around to face him.

"Okay?" he asked.

She nodded before taking his hand, leading him into the bedroom, and quietly closing the door.

Talia stepped closer to him and let her forehead fall to his chest. She wrapped her arms around his waist, tucking her chin into the side of his neck. Max enveloped her in his hold and breathed in; she was all woman, and he loved that about her. A tiny tremor prickled his skin as he quivered from her hands on his back. He knew making love wasn't an option. Talia needed to get some sleep. He'd be happy just to have her beside him.

They stood like that for a few moments before she looked up at him with her sultry, sexy eyes in the room's dim light. He glimpsed the desire, saw the wanton need to forget a night that had brought her some really sad moments.

He knew Talia was not a forward person, but she put her mouth at the open neck of his shirt, and he could feel the wetness of her lips rubbing the skin. *Fuck.* He swallowed. God, that was good. He was compliant as she trailed one hand down his back to his ass and squeezed it.

God damn it. Max had not been expecting that. He'd been hard, but now…

She looked at him with a desperate appeal in her eyes. Her pupils were large, eyes wide, and her mouth parted; those lips were seductive enough without her trying to do anything else. His hands fell to her bottom and he pulled her close so she would feel how hard he was.

"What do you want, Talia?"

"I want you, Max, only you."

He started to release her buttons. His hands were shaking, and she pushed them aside and lifted her shirt over her head. It was as if she couldn't wait for him to undo them. Today she wore a sheer pink bra, and he could see her protruding nipples through the material. While he watched, she undid the button of her jeans and slowly pulled down the zipper.

She was teasing him, and he loved it…he loved her. He wasn't even shocked at that silent admission. When she slid the jeans down her legs and he saw she had on matching panties he thought he might spontaneously combust. Max stepped forward, pulling her against him.

He fondled and squeezed her ass through the sheer material as he lifted her, leaving the jeans on the ground.

Max let her drop slowly to the floor gently so that she would feel how hard he was, and he teased her by moving her against the ridge of his erection over and over until she was breathing fast.

"Is that good?"

"Oh yes," she breathed out. "So good."

It thrilled him that he could get her so excited.

She elongated her neck and he couldn't resist the invitation. His lips settled on the softness, and he drew the skin into his mouth, gently nipping every tender spot he found.

There wasn't a part of her body that he didn't want to kiss, so he turned her around, trapping her between him and the door.

Undoing her bra, he slipped it from her arms, letting it drop to the floor. He stretched her arms above her head, palms flat to the wood. Stroking his hands down her smooth skin until he reached her breasts, he thumbed her nipples and she cried out.

Her head fell back as she gasped out, "I never thought sex could be like this."

"That's because this isn't sex," he said, letting his lips stroke the back of her neck. "It's making love."

"I feel like every nerve ending is sensitized to the limit."

"Good," he said as he palmed both hands down her stomach to the elastic of her panties. Max placed his thumbs inside the fabric to enjoy the sensation of her soft skin. Before getting down on his knees and slipping them down her legs as she stepped out of them.

His fingertips trailed up the inside of her leg ,while his lips kissed the back of her knee. Desire mingled hot in his throat. Max could feel his heart rapping at the side of his ribs, longing to be inside her. Urgent with need, he stood up and turned her around to face him, inserting a leg between hers, and she shifted in a wild move that told him she was as close as he was to an ending that would satisfy them both with utter pleasure.

"You make me crazy," Max said as he leaned down to take a nipple into his mouth. He gently scraped the hardness with his teeth, then licked the roughness of the pebbled skin. His pulse quickened with the desire that lit him up like a bonfire.

Talia cried out as she arched her back, grinding herself against his sex in a frenzied need. She was shaking; Max could feel it right through to the soles of his feet. He wanted to take her like this. He lifted her, and without persuasion, she wrapped her legs around him, holding him tightly to her.

"Take your clothes off," she gasped, her voice rough with desire.

He didn't need to be told twice. Within seconds, his clothing was in a heap on the floor.

His fingers gripped the flesh of her ass. As he kissed her parted lips, the groan she emitted thrummed through her mouth into his. His need for her was insatiable, and she responded with equal longing. He was heady with the scent of her.

"Are you okay like this?" he asked her.

She opened her eyes and gazed into his. "Yes…oh yes."

"Keep them open," he said as her lashes fell closed again. "I want to watch you."

He saw her swallow before she nodded.

Max lifted her and she pushed her hips forward, rubbing against him. He was about to thrust into her when he remembered he hadn't protected her. "Condom," he said, hovering on the precipice of pleasure.

"No need," she gasped out. "I'm on the pill."

Thank fuck for that; it would have killed him to stop now.

"Please," she said in a whisper he barely heard. "Now, I need you now." Her arms had been around his neck, but now she moved them and her fingers gripped his shoulders.

He sank into her wet folds with a harsh groan, and she gasped out his name. He stayed like that for a second, enjoying being inside her. Her needy sob was enough to set him off and he couldn't stop himself from rocking into her.

He was thrusting harder and deeper with each stroke. The feel of her warm wet sex thrummed heavenly as he felt the crescendo of waves exploding.

Her eyes were glazed over, and he was mesmerized by her…totally and completely. Talia cried out, and he could feel her clenching around him enough to make him orgasm simultaneously.

His head fell into her neck, and he held her while their bodies quivered. He savored the intimacy that only something like this could bring. At that moment, there was only him and her as they came hard, each fueling the other's climax.

Max raised his head and she smiled at him, making his heart hammer against his chest.

"That was good," she said.

"I aim to please." He grinned as she swatted him on the shoulder.

"Don't be so big-headed."

He laughed. "I wouldn't dare."

She leaned her head back, still breathing hard. "Bed?"

"Umm, bed."

He carried her to the bed and pulled back the covers, setting her down on the blue sheet. Climbing in beside her, he pulled the duvet over them.

Talia curled up against him, one of her slim, smooth legs tangled with his, and he could tell by her light breathing that she was fast asleep. He closed his eyes, thinking about how she had felt and how she came around him. It made him hard to think about it. Talia had crept her way into his heart since their first meeting. He didn't want to move her because she was now embedded in there.

"Aunty Tally, Max, he came," Charlie shouted as he switched on her lamp.

Talia sat up and groaned from the lack of sleep, thankful for getting up just fifteen minutes before to put her PJs on before he came in. Screwing up her eyes, she watched as Charlie lifted his stocking onto the bed. He seemed none the worse after yesterday's upset…was that a good thing?

"Come on, get in and we'll open it."

Charlie jumped in between her and Max. "Wake up, Max. Santa came." He shook his arm and Max opened one eye.

"Are you sure?"

"Yes, I've been downstairs and everything I left on the plate is gone, but there is a little milk left." His eyes were sparkling. "And there are a lot of presents beneath the tree."

Max laughed as he sat up and stretched.

"This stocking is massive. Can I eat some chocolate now?" He giggled, and Talia loved the sound.

Leaning down, she kissed him. "Happy birthday,

sweet boy."

"I'm six now," he said proudly.

Talia smiled. "Yes, you are."

"Can I open my stocking later?" he asked as he felt to see what was in there.

"Of course you can. Come on, let Max get dressed."

"Why doesn't he have pajamas on?"

Talia struggled to find an answer.

"Because I left them at the hotel," the man in her bed piped up.

"Oh, okay then. Hurry up, Max. I want to open all my gifts."

"Go ahead, buddy. I'll be there in a minute."

Talia laughed as he raced before her. "Watch you don't fall," she shouted after him. "The hotel?" she asked Max, tongue in cheek.

She jumped out of bed and slipped on her pajamas. Max followed her, wrapped his arms around her, and kissed her on the lips.

"Good morning, honey. Merry Christmas," he said.

She swallowed. What a difference a year makes. Talia closed her eyes, just for a moment, before opening them to his blue gaze upon her. The thrill he gave her, with hope, kindness, and a future, was there for her to see.

Talia smiled. "Good morning, gorgeous man. Merry Christmas."

They stood there just staring at each other, her hands still against his chest where his hug had squashed them.

"Aunty Tally, quick, come and see what I have."

"I'm coming," she shouted.

"Go," Max said. "We have plenty of time."

She cupped his cheek, feeling the softness of his

beard beneath her fingertips. "Yes, we do."

Leaving Max to get dressed, she hurried down the stairs to see wrapping paper everywhere, and poor Molly racing out of the room. The smell of turkey wafted past her nose, making her tummy rumble despite the earliness of the morning.

Max joined them and he lit the fire while she cleared away some of the Christmas wrappings.

After Charlie had opened all of his gifts he found some more beneath the tree. He read the labels.

"Aunty Tally, these two are for you." He handed them to her. "And these are for you, Max." Charlie gave him the gifts, then jumped up on his knee. "Can I help you?" he asked.

"You can, but first I think you have two more presents to open," he said.

"I do?" Charlie said, his face a picture of awe and excitement.

"Yes, Santa had to leave them in the kitchen because there was no room for them here."

Talia looked at him with a frown. She hadn't bought anything else.

Charlie jumped off his knee quicker than Jack Flash and hightailed it out of the room, then she heard a scream of delight.

"You weren't the only one up early." Max winked at her as they followed the whoops coming from her nephew.

Before she could get to the kitchen, Charlie came cycling into the hallway on a bike with stabilizers. Talia's heart thumped like a drum as she sat on the bottom stair and watched him.

How on earth did Max know Charlie had been

dreaming of a new bike?

Max moved in front of her on his hunches. "Charlie told me about his bike, stolen from the garden, and he wanted a new one from Santa.

But you told him that although he'd been an exceptionally good boy this year you didn't think he'd be getting one because he was getting lots of other things." He took her hands. "I hope it was okay?" It was the first time she'd seen an uncertain look on his face.

Talia gave a shaky smile, she was so overwhelmed by him. She cupped both his cheeks in her hands. "Max Harvey, you are the kindest man I have ever met. Thank you."

"Are you two going to kiss again? Yuck, yuck," Charlie said with his helmet on and sitting astride the bike.

Max's eyes dropped to her mouth. "You'll understand when you're older, Charlie." And he kissed her gently on the lips.

* * * *

The day was long but one of, if not the happiest she'd ever spent. Everything from the early morning to the freezing cold watching her nephew on his bike and Max helping him. That evening when she and Max put a sleepy boy to bed, he drew Alfie close to him and lay on his side as she was tucking him in.

"Aunty Tally?"

"Yes, honey." She sat on the bed next to him.

"I'm sad that Mummy has gone."

"Me too," she said, smoothing his hair back from his brow.

"But she will be much happier, won't she?"

Talia nodded. "I think so."

There was silence for a few seconds. Max was standing behind her with his hand on her shoulder.

"Can I call you Mummy now?"

A tear splashed to her cheek, and she drew up a shallow breath. "Yes, honey, you can."

"And my other Mummy won't mind?"

"No, baby, she won't." She leaned down and buried her lips in his hair. "Night night, honey."

She stood up as his eyes closed, and she turned to Max who held onto her tightly.

"You okay?" he whispered.

"Yes."

"And if you and Max get married, can I call him Daddy?"

The question embarrassed Talia and she didn't know how to respond, but she didn't have to say anything because Max let go of her to lean down and kiss the little boy.

"Yes, bud, I'd like that."

"Night, Mummy. Night, Max."

They both left the room and Max followed her downstairs into the living room where he shut the door behind him. Talia smiled at him. "Well, that was emotional."

She didn't know whether she should say something about the 'getting married' quip Charlie had said or not, and in the end, she decided to say nothing.

Max reached into his pocket and drew out a small box wrapped in gold paper. The wrapping had red ribbon around it, and the glitter caught the Christmas lights. Talia's heartbeat quickened as he handed it to her.

Her brows lifted in surprise. "We gave each other presents this morning."

"I know, but this is just an extra one for you." He flashed her a smile, but she thought she saw a little anxiety in those eyes. Max drew her close, tipping her face to his. "You must know by now that I love you?"

"No," she said with a shake of her head. "I hoped, but I didn't know." Her mouth was dry and she had to swallow several times before she took a deep, steadying breath. "I love you too," she said as her lips quivered.

"Thank God for that. I was worried for a moment that I'd read the situation between us wrong." His voice was low from his throat and shook with emotion. "Open the box," he said, his smile lazy and loving.

Her stomach turned over as she stepped back a little, and with shaking fingers, she pulled off the paper. A huge amber stone with flecks of black in it lit up like a fire. "It's beautiful," she said.

"Just like your eyes," he said as he took it from her and slipped it on her finger. Max's eyes lingered on hers.

"Is this real?" she asked, feeling euphoric.

"Yes." He bent his head, and his mouth hovered above hers. "I love you and Charlie. You are what I've been waiting for, and I knew it the minute I set eyes on you."

"This might be your last chance to make a beeline for the exit," she said, but she wasn't joking.

"I'm one hundred and fifty percent sure I'm happy right where I am." His gaze dropped to her mouth. "I love you, baby. Forever and always you'll be mine." He pulled her to him and kissed her long and thoroughly, leaving no doubt about how he felt.

"I love you too," she whispered

There was a noise behind them and they both turned around to see Charlie standing there. "Does this mean I can call Max daddy now?" he asked, his eyes bright.

"You sure can, buddy," Max said, picking him up. He tucked Talia into his side and brought them together.

"Now we are a family," Charlie said.

Talia looked at Max, the love of her life, and nodded. "Yes, honey, we are."

"Merry Christmas, Mummy and Daddy."

A word about the author…

Author Dilys J Carnie loves to write, usually contemporary romance, sometimes with a bit of suspense thrown in for good measure.

If she isn't in her office pounding the keys, she's settling into her favorite chair to read a book from one of her many best-loved authors.

Dilys is the proud mum of two grown-up children and two grandchildren.

She lives on the coast of Wales in the United Kingdom.

It is only two hundred steps to the beach from her home, where she lives with her cat Molly.

http://www.dilysjcarnie.com

Thank you for purchasing
this publication of The Wild Rose Press, Inc.

For questions or more information
contact us at
info@thewildrosepress.com.

The Wild Rose Press, Inc.
www.thewildrosepress.com